RECAPTURED BY THE CRIME LORD

CRIME LORD SERIES, BOOK 2

MIA KNIGHT

COPYRIGHT

DEDICATION

To the authors who nourished my love for stories and taught me at a young age how to dream.

1

LYLA

Lyla Dalton strolled along a creek in Montana, willing the tranquility of her surroundings to ease her troubled mind. She didn't sleep much anymore. No place, no matter how isolated or beautiful, made her feel safe. Most days, she felt like a walking zombie—no thoughts or feeling penetrated the thick layer of white noise that shielded her from the outside world. Other times, she felt so much she couldn't stand it.

Once upon a time, she and her cousin, Carmen, led privileged lives with men who loved them. That life shattered when Carmen's husband and Lyla's future father-in-law Manny were murdered. Lyla had been mutilated by the same killer who was interrupted before he could finish her off.

Eight stab wounds and three slashes over six inches in length marred her abdomen. The raised edges of her scars brushed against the thin material of her shirt. The horror she felt watching merciless criminals break every bone in Manny's body and the memory of the blade sinking into her chest made her sick. She wouldn't forget the sound of

Manny's screams abruptly cutting off as he drowned in his own blood.

Lyla stopped on the trail and put her hands on her knees while she waited for the nausea to pass. In the wake of the tragedies, her ex tried to throw the cops off his bloody trail and she and her cousin took off. Carmen withdrew money from her bank account, bought an RV, and they went on the road. They periodically stayed in motels or rented cabins when they needed a break from the close confines of the RV, but they paid for everything with cash so there was no trail. If they felt the urge to move on, they did so. They lived cautiously, avoiding big cities and populated areas. On the rare occasions when Lyla was forced to interact with others, her composure creaked under the strain of trying to appear normal.

She settled on a flat-topped rock along the creek and tipped her face up to the sun and took a deep breath of clean, fresh air. Montana was beautiful and had been their home for about a week now. She wished the warmth from the sun would touch her cold soul, which had holes in it that would never heal. Despite the fact they had been on the road for a year and a half, she still felt as fragile as she'd been the day Manny was murdered. Knowing people in the world were capable of that level of brutality kept her up at night.

Carmen told her that her ex-fiancee, Gavin, went to jail for money laundering, the only charge they were able to pin on him since they didn't have enough evidence to try him for murder. Lyla didn't ask how long he would be in jail. She didn't care. When she woke in the hospital with fatal stab wounds, Gavin didn't ask about Manny's murder or her well-being. All he wanted was information on the men he was hunting. Since the men involved in Manny's murder wore masks, she had nothing to give him and hadn't seen him again. Gavin blamed her for Vinny's death and had been cold and remote while she lay held together with stitches and staples in the hospital bed. She focused on getting better and left the moment she could with Carmenby distracting the men so they could make their getaway. Slowly, her body mended but not her spirit.

Lyla rose after the sun heat her skin and started back toward the cabin. After surviving the traumatic attack and skipping out on physiotherapy, she forced herself to explore to strengthen her body and to make sure they weren't followed. Branches snapped beneath her sneakers. Her eyes swept the forest for bears, rattlesnakes, coyotes, or cougars. She carried a pistol to defend herself against wildlife and any man who thought two women traveling alone would be fair game. Carmen taught her how to use a gun. Lyla became a decent shot but hadn't had the chance to put her new skills to the test.

She left the path as she made her way back to their rented cabin and heard voices up ahead. She cleared the trees and took in the bizarre scene. A small army of SUVs and men were in the clearing. For a second, she thought they were police officers until she registered that they were in suits and not uniforms.

A large man prowled through the crowd. The other suits gave way to him. Even across the distance, Lyla sensed the air crackling around him. Fear shot through her along with a healthy dose of adrenaline. Even as her legs tensed to run, the man stopped in his tracks and spotted her. Her finely honed survival instinct kicked in. She whirled and ran back along the path as fast as she could. Between the burble of the creek and the sound of her heart beat, she couldn't hear anyone behind her, but she didn't stop. Her mind was a blank slate of fear and denial. No, he couldn't be here.

There was no warning. One moment she was running headlong down the path, and the next, something hit her hard from behind. She landed against a hard body as they tumbled to the ground. She tried to wrench away as they rolled, fighting tooth and nail. He spoke, but she couldn't hear over the ringing in her ears. She reached for her gun, but he disarmed her without effort and pinned her hands over her head. He sat on her stomach, taking her breath away. She stared up at Gavin Pyre, the man she'd run from twice in her lifetime. He had an angular face, slick black hair, and blazing amber eyes. His gray suit was now covered in dead leaves, twigs, and dirt.

"Stop it," he hissed.

She panted beneath him, unable to find her voice. How did he find them? What was he doing here? What did he want? He didn't look like he just got out of jail. He looked as pristine and polished as always.

Gavin tucked her pistol into his trousers at the small of his back. He rose and hauled her up with him. Before she had time to register that he was really here and touching her as if he had every right to, Gavin began to march her along the path back to the cabins. Fear and rage collided, giving her the strength she needed to break his grip on her. Her mind screamed at her to get as far away from him as possible.

She left the path and began to zigzag through the forest. She didn't gain more than a dozen paces before Gavin caught up with her. He grabbed her arm and swung her around. Lyla went for his face with her nails. He dodged and twisted one hand behind her back, but Lyla wasn't deterred. She balled her fist and clipped his jaw before he restrained her other hand. She glared up at him, chest pumping, daring him to retaliate.

A muscle clenched in Gavin's jaw. "Don't."

"I hate you!" she shouted and struggled to no avail. "Why are you here?"

"Because you are."

She lunged at him, hoping to unbalance him so she could make another run for it. Gavin made an impatient sound and shoved her in front of him with her hands locked behind her back. He propelled her forward at a pace fast enough that she didn't have time to struggle. She had to focus on her footing on the uneven terrain. Gavin didn't let up for a second.

When they walked into the clearing, Gavin's men fell silent. Under their scrutiny, sanity reasserted itself, and she looked at Gavin. Ice blue eyes clashed with gold. He hesitated before he released her, but gripped her arm in a painful hold she couldn't break. She didn't struggle as he led her into the cabin. She came to a dead stop when she found Gavin's head of security standing over her cousin with a gun. Carmen, once the arm candy of one of the wealthiest men in Las Vegas, was unrecognizable. She chopped off her long blonde locks and wore jeans and hiking boots instead of cutout dresses and hooker heels.

"What the fuck are you doing, Blade?" Lyla demanded and tried to get to her cousin, but Gavin held her back.

"How's it going?" Blade asked pleasantly.

"I'm assuming Carmen is the one who helped you escape the first time," Gavin said.

Lyla didn't answer. What difference did it make?

"I've been searching for you two for six months. If it wasn't for your beauty, you probably would have gone unnoticed and untraceable forever," Gavin said and gestured to someone outside.

An older gentleman walked into the cabin with a Bible clasped to his chest. He was sweating profusely and eyed Gavin and Blade as if they were savages. Gavin turned to Lyla with a placid expression that was completely at odds with the grip he had on her arm and the rage glittering in his eyes.

"I'm assuming you don't want anything to happen to Carmen," Gavin said.

Lyla stiffened. "What are you talking about?"

"You care for your cousin, right?"

Lyla didn't answer. Gavin reached into his pocket and pulled out a blue diamond engagement ring. She felt as if she had been doused in ice water. She had a vivid recollection of slipping it off her finger in the hospital room and hearing it roll across the floor. She never thought she would see it again. Seeing the ring after all this time felt like a slap across the face. Lyla tried to get away, but he wasn't in the mood to allow a tantrum. He used his considerable strength to restrain her and leaned down so their faces were less than an inch apart.

"You don't want me to hurt your cousin," he said.

"What is wrong with you?" This was a nightmare. Gavin couldn't be here in Montana with her old engagement ring threatening Carmen's life.

"Do you want me to hurt her?" Gavin asked.

"No!"

"Then do as I say."

Gavin growled when she clenched her hand into a fist. He forced her hand to unfurl, and despite her attempts to evade, he slipped the ring on her finger. Gavin clasped their hands together and turned to the man with the Bible.

"Begin," Gavin ordered.

The stranger avoided Lyla's gaze as he began to speak.

"We are gathered here today to witness the union of Gavin Pyre and Lyla Dalton."

"No!" Lyla shouted as her knees buckled.

Gavin wrapped an arm around her waist and hauled her against him. When Carmen opened her mouth to protest, Blade clucked his tongue to discourage her and pressed the gun against her temple.

"Lyla, don't do this. He can't make you," Carmen shouted.

"Keep going," Gavin barked at the pastor who was clearly terrified. He leaned close and whispered in her ear, "You want Carmen to come out of this alive, then you agree with everything he says."

"How can you threaten Carmen? She lost her husband!" Lyla glared up at him. "You remember Vinny?"

Gavin's implacable expression didn't soften. "Twice now Carmen's taken you from me. I should kill her for all this wasted time."

"Carmen has nothing to do with our relationship, and you wouldn't hurt her."

"Want to put it to the test?"

No, she didn't want to test him. Gavin didn't bluff and his bone-crushing grip suggested he wasn't in a teasing mood. "Why are you doing this?"

"Gavin Pyre, in taking Lyla Dalton to be your wife, do you promise to honor, love, and cherish her in sickness and in health, in poverty and in wealth, in hardship and in blessing, until death do you part?" the pastor asked in a quavering voice.

"I do," Gavin said without looking away from Lyla.

"And Lyla Dalton, in taking Gavin Pyre to be your husband," the pastor continued.

Lyla shook her head. Gavin clasped her face between his hands to stop the motion.

"We've wasted too much time," he said.

Her eyes burned with tears. "Every night, I hear your father screaming. I can't get it out of my head. I won't go back to that life."

"You have no choice. You gave yourself to me. There's no out for either of us. You'll have to live with me, and I with you."

"I made my choice," she said, gesturing around her at the cabin. "I choose to live without you."

"Not acceptable," he bit out.

"Lyla Dalton, do you take Gavin Pyre to be your husband?" the pastor asked tentatively, clearly dreading her answer.

Gavin gripped the back of her neck. "Say yes."

"No—" she began, but Gavin covered her mouth with his.

She was too stunned to defend herself against the sensual assault. His tongue swept into her mouth, claiming her as his, a claim he revoked the moment he stepped back into the criminal underworld. Lyla dug her nails into his chest, desperate for air and space. Gavin was overwhelming —always had been, always would be. She could feel how tense he was, a coiled spring ready to erupt. He was a law unto himself. When he pulled back, her lips tingled.

"Say yes and I won't punish Carmen for taking you from me," he said in a low voice only she could hear.

"How can you punish her?"

"No one comes between us."

"*You* let business come between us."

"Say yes," he ordered, so close that all she could see were his burning gold eyes, demanding her compliance.

"Clearly," Carmen said sarcastically, "she doesn't want him."

"Blade," Gavin snapped.

Blade twisted Carmen's arm behind her back, and she let out a cry of pain. Lyla tried to get away from Gavin, but he held her in place. Blade forced Carmen toward the front door with the gun to her temple.

"What is he going to do to her?" Lyla demanded.

"Say yes or you won't see her again."

"What's wrong with you?"

"Say it now, goddammit," Gavin said through clenched teeth.

"Yes, I do," Lyla said quickly, heart thundering in her chest.

Blade paused in the doorway and winked at her. She wanted to kill him.

"By the power vested in me, I now pronounce you married," the pastor said and wiped the sweat out of his eyes.

"Where's the marriage license?" Gavin asked.

The pastor presented the piece of paper and offered a pen. Gavin handed the pen to her. She signed, eyes on Carmen who looked as if hell warmed over. If looks could kill, Gavin and Blade would be dead. Blade signed as the witness and escorted Carmen outside.

"Where is he taking her?" Lyla demanded. "You promised you wouldn't—"

"He's taking her to her mother," Gavin said shortly as he pushed a diamond wedding band on her finger. It fit snugly against the blue diamond engagement ring. Before her bemused eyes, he pulled out a gold wedding band and placed it on his left ring finger.

In the span of thirty minutes, Gavin Pyre once again turned her life upside down. Without another word, Gavin led her out of the cabin. He placed her in the back seat of an SUV and climbed in next to her. She sat there in shock, staring straight ahead.

"Where are we going?" she asked.

"Home."

Even though she had been expecting that answer, she shut her eyes against the flood of tears. Las Vegas, where she didn't feel safe and her nightmares took place in real life. Just the thought of going back made her sick.

"I can't," she whispered.

"You will."

"Why?"

Gavin didn't answer.

"I can't take this," she said as tears filled her eyes. "How many times do I have to tell you? I want no part of your life. I hate you."

"Lyla, stop."

"No! You just show up, tackle me, threaten to hurt my cousin, and force me to marry you. Who the hell do you think you are?"

Gavin turned toward her. If she could run, she would have. Although Gavin had always been a bit scary, there was a quality to him now that made him seem even more menacing.

"I'm your husband," he said in a soft voice that sent chills up her spine. "Don't forget it."

When she tried to scoot away, he tightened his hold, anchoring her to his side. It didn't take long to reach a small, private airstrip. Her stomach plummeted when she saw

Gavin's private jet, the same one that had collected her from Maine almost two years ago. Gavin led her on board. She was relieved to see Carmen there, unhurt. Lyla broke away from Gavin and ran to Carmen who hugged her tight.

"Girl, are you okay?" Carmen whispered.

She didn't answer. She wasn't sure how she felt. Being legally bound to Gavin wasn't 'okay,' and Carmen knew it. A hand twisted in the back of her shirt and inexorably pulled until she was out of her cousin's embrace. She landed against a rock-hard chest. Muscular arms wrapped her possessively close.

"You have some nerve," Carmen began, hands on hips. "You have no idea what she's been through because of you!"

"I'll let you live out of respect for Vinny," Gavin said, his icy voice easily cutting through Carmen's outraged one.

Carmen paled, and when Lyla looked up, she could see why. Something that looked very close to hatred flared in Gavin's eyes.

"You must've been grief stricken and temporarily insane to remove Lyla from my protection to go driving around the United States with my father's killer on the loose," Gavin said. "Don't mistake my leniency toward you for forgiveness. I'm sending you to your mother. Your father passed two months ago."

Lyla jerked. Uncle Louie died? It was another shock on top of too many. Carmen staggered back, clearly stunned.

"He had a heart attack. You'll stay with your mom. I sold your house and put a freeze on what's left of your money, so you don't do anything stupid. You need money for something, you need to go through me," Gavin said in a clipped voice.

"That's *my* money!" Carmen shouted.

"Not anymore."

In contrast, Gavin's voice was whisper quiet and way more effective.

"You've shown that you're reckless and thoughtless. Until I'm satisfied, you won't have access to your money or Lyla."

"You smug bastard! You have no idea what you did to her," Carmen said as she flushed with rage. "Have you seen her scars? Have you heard her screaming at night? Were you there to hold her when she cried? Do you know what happened the day your father died? No, you don't. I wish I didn't know, but I do. You broke your promise and left her alone in a hospital bed when she needed you. You went off to chase those bastards, so I took your place. She asked me to get her out, so I did. You think she would have been safe with your expensive security detail?" Carmen sneered. "If she was so safe, your father would still be alive and she wouldn't be scarred for life."

Lyla felt his body go rigid a moment before his fist flashed out. Blade deflected Gavin's punch before it connected with Carmen's face. The air around them went electric as Gavin went apeshit and launched himself at her cousin. Guards went flying and blood sprayed the luxurious carpet as Gavin's security team tried to restrain him. Flight attendants screamed and ran off the jet. Lyla caught a glimpse of Gavin's face, contorted with blind rage. It made her clammy with fear. It took nearly ten minutes for his men to pin him down. Lyla couldn't see him, buried as he was beneath a pile of men. Blade knelt on the ground to talk sense into him.

When Gavin resurfaced, everyone watched him like a ticking bomb. Although his expression was impassive, no one trusted his control. Several men stood in front of Carmen with their hands on their weapons. Gavin's eyes fixed on Lyla, and he moved toward her. Lyla backed up, but there was nowhere to run. He caught her up in his arms, walked to the back of the jet, and locked them in a private room. Even as he dumped her on the bed and came down on top of her, she heard the engine rev. Gavin tucked his head under her chin and settled his body on hers.

"Get off me!" Lyla shouted and pounded his shoulders, but he didn't budge. "You could've killed her."

No response from Gavin.

"You're out of control."

"Going to jail will do that to you," he said, lips moving against her skin as he spoke.

Lyla hesitated before she asked, "How long were you in?"

"A year. I've been out six months, looking for you."

"You didn't have to. I'm fine," she said.

"So what Carmen said isn't true?"

She didn't answer. She heard the low murmur of voices on the other side of the door, but no one interrupted them as the jet gained speed and lifted off. Gavin showed no signs of moving, so she blocked him out and stared at the ceiling. It took nearly half an hour for her to process everything that happened, but two points stood out amongst the rest. One, she was now married to Gavin Pyre. Two, she was going back to where it all began.

2

GAVIN

GAVIN CROSSED THE CLEARING. He couldn't believe they were in Montana. If he weren't grasping at straws, he would have thought the tip that brought them here was a mistake. It never occurred to him that Carmen would be able to live in an RV. She was high maintenance, materialistic, and the furthest thing from a girl scout. Lyla, on the other hand, he could imagine on the road. She wanted a simple life, and this was as ordinary as it got.

The tip paid off. Carmen was here, but where was Lyla? Carmen claimed Lyla had gone to town, but he didn't believe her. She took Lyla from him not once but twice. He barely refrained from snapping her neck. He spent sleepless nights in jail being tortured by visions of Lyla being murdered in one hundred different ways. *Where was she?*

He was halfway across the clearing when he felt a tingle along the back of his neck. He turned, looked past the ranks of men, and saw a slight figure in jeans and a long sleeve shirt. A slight woman wore a trucker's hat low over her face, but that didn't disguise the exquisite face, generous mouth, and ice blue eyes. Even across the distance, he sensed her panic. He opened his mouth to call out to her but didn't bother when she turned and ran.

He shoved through his men and took off after her. Adrenaline shot through his system. He had been looking for her for six months. He wasn't about to let her out of his sight. She was fast, but he was faster. She kept to the trail, which made it easier for him. He gained on her, eyes never leaving the golden ponytail streaming behind her like a cape.

When he was close enough, he lunged and wrapped his arms around her. He took the brunt of the fall before he rolled and pinned her beneath him. He wanted to see her face and look into her eyes, but Lyla was fighting him like a wild animal.

"Stop, Lyla!" he said, which made no impact whatsoever.

Her eyes were blind with panic and fear. He saw a flash of silver and knocked the gun out of her hand. At least Carmen had the brains to teach her how to defend herself. He rested his weight on her abdomen and pinned her hands over her head. The impact she had on his senses was devastating. He couldn't decide whether to strangle or make love to her. She was thinner than he remembered, and the sheer terror in her eyes gutted him.

"Stop it," he hissed.

He was close to losing it. If they stayed out here any longer, he would bury himself in her to make sure this wasn't a dream. He hauled her up, eyes averted, and started back toward the cabin. Lyla twisted out of his hold and began to dodge through the trees. Fear made him move faster than he had in his life. He swung her around and wasn't quick enough to avoid the blow. The force of the punch surprised him. It jerked his head to the side and made him realize how much she changed. Lyla didn't do violence, but the woman looking back at him had nothing to lose. She was capable of anything.

"I hate you!" she shouted as she struggled. "Why are you here?"

"Because you are."

The last time he saw her in the hospital, he'd been a prick. Worse than a prick, but that couldn't be helped. He'd been working day and night to find the culprit who murdered his father and tried to kill her. He couldn't afford to sit by her hospital bed while the cops were breathing down his neck. The way she looked at him that day haunted him. He would make it up to her, but first, he had other things to see to.

He marched her back to the cabin, pushing her at a merciless pace; his need to bind her to him a drum beat in his blood. He was acting crazy and didn't care. Lyla was alive, and he wouldn't let go until she was legally his. When they entered the cabin, he was grimly satisfied to find Blade holding Carmen at gunpoint. Lyla stopped in her tracks. He was glad she grasped the situation so quickly.

"What the fuck are you doing, Blade?" Lyla asked and tried to go toward the traitor.

"How's it going?" Blade asked.

"I'm assuming Carmen is the one who helped you escape the first time," he said but didn't wait for an answer. "I've been searching for you two for six months. If it wasn't for your beauty, you probably would have gone unnoticed and untraceable forever." The trucker who tipped them off went into great detail about Carmen and Lyla's attributes. He allowed the trucker to live with the memory of them since he would never lay eyes on them again.

He caught a whiff of Lyla's scent. He shook his head to keep himself focused. He would indulge later. Now, they had shit to settle. He gestured to the pastor and mentally braced as he looked down at Lyla. "I'm assuming you don't want anything to happen to Carmen."

Ice blue eyes widened. "What are you talking about?"

"You care for your cousin, right?"

He pulled out the engagement ring, the only thing she left behind in the hospital room. He saw recognition and rage rip across her face before she fought him. He had to use considerable strength to restrain her. He could feel the combined distress of both women, but he couldn't back down. Not now.

"You don't want me to hurt your cousin," he said.

"What is wrong with you?"

She looked at him as if he was a monster, and even as that sent a shaft of pain through his chest, he continued with his plan. "Do you want me to hurt her?"

"No!"

"Then do as I say."

He had to make a conscious effort not to hurt her as he struggled to get the ring on her finger. When he succeeded, he clasped their hands together and ignored her twitching fingers. He ordered the pastor to get on with it and caught Lyla before she hit the floor. He wanted to strangle Carmen when she said Lyla had a choice. Lyla *didn't* have a choice. Neither of them did, they just didn't know it yet. When Lyla said Vinny's name, guilt clawed at him.

The pastor prompted him for those two words that would bind Lyla to him. He didn't hesitate. "I do."

The predator in him lunged to the surface when Lyla refused to take him as her husband.

"We've wasted too much time," he said and felt his insides twist when her eyes filled with tears.

"Every night, I hear your father screaming. I can't get it out of my head. I won't go back to that life."

He had to beat back the murderous haze. He focused on her for all he was worth. He couldn't lose it, not when he was so close to his goal. "You have no choice. You gave yourself to me. There's no out for either of us. You'll have to live with me, and I with you."

"I made my choice. I choose to live without you."

"Not acceptable." Didn't she understand that?

"Lyla Dalton, do you take Gavin Pyre to be your husband?" the pastor asked.

All he needed was two words. She would give them to him. He gripped the back of her neck. "Say yes."

"No—" she began, and he lost it.

He covered her mouth with his and swept his tongue into her mouth, reclaiming her. Her nails dug into his chest, but he didn't release her. She tasted the same—sweet with a hint of rebellion. When he pulled back, he was pleased to see that her lips were swollen and she looked stunned.

"Say yes and I won't punish Carmen for taking you from me."

"How can you punish her?"

"No one comes between us." Didn't she know that? Not that fucking IT guy she met in Maine, not Carmen, not her parents. No one.

"*You* let business come between us."

"Say yes."

"Clearly, she doesn't want him," Carmen said.

His temper roared to life. If he weren't holding Lyla, he would have put his hands on her worthless cousin.

"Blade," he bit out and noted Lyla's panic. If he was a decent human being, he wouldn't take away her free will, wouldn't blackmail her into marrying him. He wasn't a decent human being. "Say yes or you won't see her again."

"What's wrong with you?" she whispered.

He wanted her fucking agreement. If he brought her asshole father, he could have filled him with bullets, which would make Lyla agree faster and satisfy his bloodthirsty mood.

"Say it now, goddammit," Gavin said through clenched teeth, dimly aware of Blade shoving Carmen toward the door with a gun to her temple.

"Yes, I do," Lyla said.

While she signed the marriage license, he slid his father's wedding ring onto his finger. That's where it would stay until the day he died, just like his father. In the back of the SUV, he tried to calm himself with the knowledge that she was here and legally bound to him. The savage creature inside him bared its teeth when Lyla ran to Carmen once they boarded the jet. He twisted his hand in the back of Lyla's shirt and pulled her against him.

"You have some nerve," Carmen began, hands on hips. "You have no idea what she's been through because of you!"

"I'll let you live out of respect for Vinny," he said, hoping she would shut the fuck up so he could keep himself under control. "You must've been grief stricken and temporarily insane to remove Lyla from my protection to go driving around the United States with my father's killer on the loose. Don't mistake my leniency toward you for forgiveness. I'm sending you to your mother. Your father passed two months ago."

He should have felt bad for revealing that her father died in such an abrupt matter, but he didn't. His killer instinct urged him to eradicate anyone who got between him and Lyla. Every word out of Carmen's mouth fanned the icy rage in his belly. The only thing that kept him sane was the feel of Lyla's body pressed against his.

"You smug bastard! You have no idea what you did to her. Have you seen her scars? Have you heard her screaming at night? Were you there to hold her when she cried? Do you know what happened the day your father died? No, you don't. I wish I didn't know, but I do. You broke your promise and left her alone in a hospital bed when she needed you. You went off to chase those bastards, so I took your place. She asked me to get her out, so I did. You think she would have been safe with your expensive security detail? If she was so safe, your father would still be alive and she wouldn't be scarred for life."

He could still hear the echo of gunfire as he stepped into his father's mansion that day. Men were everywhere. His eyes swept the room for his father and Lyla and landed on two bodies on the floor covered in blood. Neither moved. Even as his mind refused to believe what he was seeing, he knew it was them. The memory fired his blood, triggering every aggressive instinct he possessed. Annihilating the masked men who weren't fast enough to escape his wrath did nothing to assuage his need for blood. Nothing would until the man who murdered his father and Vinny stopped breathing. They couldn't exist on the same planet.

Gavin wasn't aware that he moved until the smell of fresh blood stung the air. The feel of his fists connecting with flesh made him hungry for more. It wasn't until he was buried beneath a pile of sweaty men that he could think rationally. Fuck. He lunged at Carmen, and his men had to step in. Lyla wouldn't forgive this.

"Get the fuck off me," he ordered.

No one moved until Blade reinforced the order. Everyone knew he was off his rocker. Fuck. He rose and searched the jet for his wife. Covered in dirt and milky pale, she stared at him as if he was the devil incarnate. Maybe he was, but she was stuck with him. He ignored his throbbing fists, hauled her into his arms, and walked into the room in the back of the jet. Lyla gasped when he dumped her on the bed and splayed his revved-up body over hers.

He absorbed the feel of her. She was alive and trembling. He rehearsed what he would say when he found her again—apologies, threats, and promises—but his carefully crafted speeches didn't pass his lips. How could he forget that she made him feel like a fucking caveman? He wanted to control, devour, and possess. Lyla Dalton was his.

He tried to eradicate the lethal fury pumping through him. He could have broken Carmen's jaw or worse. He wrapped himself around Lyla, wanting to be absorbed by her. Carmen's accusations butchered his already mangled conscience. He wasn't completely sane. Had he ever been? Maybe not. After witnessing what those savages did to his father and Lyla, he wasn't sure he ever would be. The need to hunt, to kill was a compulsion he couldn't get rid of. He lay on top of Lyla, hoping her presence would calm him the fuck down. He inhaled the scent of her skin—soap, the outdoors, and fear. He had things to say to her. He should cradle her on his lap and beg for forgiveness, but he couldn't move or speak. His mind and body couldn't accept she was here after another disappearing act. Never again. She would never get away from him again. He would make sure of it this time. He fucked up too many times to count, but he wouldn't let her give up on him. If there was a woman in the world who could save him, it was the one he just made his wife.

His hands moved up and down her sides, reacquainting her with his touch. He heard the hitch in her breathing and ignored her struggles to get free. He couldn't look into her eyes, not after seeing his own reflection. He would remake himself, be the man his father and Lyla believed he could be. He would do whatever it took to make her happy, but right now, he couldn't do anything but let his flesh imprint on hers and soak her in.

"Get off me! You could've killed her."

He could have. It didn't even register in his mind that he was going to strike. He reacted without thinking. He wasn't going to admit that to her.

"You're out of control."

"Going to jail will do that to you." Being caged when he should have been hunting for the new crime lord drove him insane. Not knowing where Lyla was caused him to use the walls of his cell as a punching bag.

"How long were you in?"

"A year. I've been out six months, looking for you."

"You didn't have to. I'm fine."

Fine after watching his father be tortured to death and being stabbed multiple times? There were shadows in her eyes that would never fade. "So what Carmen said isn't true?"

She didn't answer. He was fine with that. He had her where he wanted her. Her scent lulled him as nothing else in the world could. He was in danger of drifting off when she spoke.

"Gavin, let me up."

"I need this." How could he tell her that her presence was the only thing keeping him in one piece?

"I can't do this," she whispered.

"You can." She had to.

"You can't just show up and take over," she said as she slapped his shoulders.

He didn't bother to contradict her since that's exactly what he'd done and would continue to do without mercy. At seventeen, she claimed him. It didn't matter what happened in the intervening years. What was left of his soul craved her. She had loved him once. She would again.

"What do you want from me?" she asked.

"Everything you promised me."

She strained beneath him but had no hope of jostling him. He weighed twice what she did, and he was solid muscle.

"You broke your promise to me, Gavin!"

He had, and it ate at him. If he had listened to her, his father would still be alive and she wouldn't have run from him again. "Everything's going to be different this time around," he said against the smooth skin of her throat.

"It doesn't feel like it. You blackmailed me into marrying you, and now you're holding me down."

"When we get home, I swear it'll be different." He couldn't talk here. He wanted to be in their home, in their bed when he spilled his guts. Knowing that everyone was on the other side of the door made him feel crowded and crazed.

He only gave a shit about three people on this planet, and two of them had been murdered on his watch. He watched the life drain out of the man's eyes who shot Vinny only to find out that he was a pawn of the new crime lord. He dreamed of ways to torture the man who had murdered his father. Some called him a psychopath. Maybe he was. He didn't have a wide range of emotions unless it involved the small circle of those he loved. With Vinny and his father gone, Lyla was his only anchor. He couldn't function without knowing where she was. He hoped she was ready to take him on because she was the only one who could.

3

LYLA

LYLA SPENT the two-hour flight from Montana to Nevada in bed with Gavin, but neither of them slept. Every word out of his mouth sounded as if it pained him. Her struggles and complaints made no difference, so she stayed prone, wondering why God hated her so much. When the plane landed, Gavin didn't move until Blade knocked on the door.

"She's gone," Blade said.

"Who's gone?" Lyla demanded, knowing full well he was referring to Carmen. "Where did she go?"

"To her mother." Gavin sat up and paused as if he needed to get his bearings.

"Are you on something?" It would explain his psycho behavior.

"I wish," he muttered and rose. "Let's go."

Lyla stretched and didn't flinch when Gavin took her hand. After having him lay on top of her for nearly two hours, handholding was nothing. He led her off the jet and into the dry desert heat. Las Vegas. She couldn't escape Sin City; it kept calling her back.

Gavin led her to the waiting SUV and climbed in the

back with her. He wore sunglasses, so she couldn't read his expression, and she had no idea what was going on in his head. If they crossed paths again, she expected him to grovel at her feet or be the remote killer he'd been when she left Las Vegas. The man who forced her into marriage was neither. Something was brewing beneath the surface, and she didn't want to find out what it was.

When they reached Gavin's home, she stepped out of the SUV but made no move to enter. Gavin propelled her inside. She gave their surroundings a cursory glance. Nothing had changed. Had she expected it to? Being here made her want to weep with frustration and rage.

"Shower," Gavin said and led her upstairs.

When he pulled her into the bathroom, she yanked her hand away and crossed her arms. She wanted a shower, but she wasn't going to take one with *him*.

"We're not going to shower together," she snapped.

He opened his mouth to argue and then hesitated. "I guess it wouldn't be a good idea. We need to talk."

"Yes, we do," she agreed.

Abruptly, he stripped out of his ruined suit. She turned away, but not before she caught a glimpse of his incredible body in the mirror. He was even more muscular than before. He looked more like a boxer than the CEO of Pyre Casinos. *Was* he still the CEO? He went to jail, and Vinny's death left an opening for COO, so where did that leave the company? How did Gavin get out of the murder charges? Apparently, he was still wealthy since he had security, the jet, and the mansion. Questions she refused to think about for the past year and a half bubbled to the surface. She didn't think about Gavin because it hurt too fucking much. Now, there was no way to avoid him.

That was the thing about Gavin. Being with him was like

riding a roller coaster—unexpected turns, drops, and rolls. She wasn't sure whether to hang on, raise her hands in the air, or let go. Her personality demanded she let go and she had—*twice*. Gavin had the opposite opinion, which is why she was in this opulent bathroom again with a priceless blue diamond ring on her finger. Gavin shocked her out of her sleepwalking state and caused her emotions to bubble up inside her. She wanted to go back to a half-life where she wasn't living or dead. No bumps in the road, no drama, and no Gavin Pyre. She didn't want friction. Gavin was a stick of dynamite.

She left the bathroom and went to the walk-in closet. Once again, she was struck by the fact that nothing had changed. Gavin was a stubborn bastard. She'd left him twice, and he still kept her clothes and shoes? Most men would have gone on a rampage and tossed her shit out. Not Gavin. What would Manny say about that? He would probably puff his chest out and beam with pride.

The stabbing pain in her chest made her keel over. Living a half-life also meant she didn't have to think about Manny. The only thing she pondered on the road was the next destination. She refused to let herself think about Vegas or the Pyres. Now all she could think about was the father she lost. She didn't realize she was sobbing until wet arms wrapped around her. She broke free and whirled to find Gavin with a towel around his waist, water streaming everywhere. For the first time that day, she really looked at him. He may have bulked up, but there was a stark quality to his muscles, as if he was working out more than he was eating. As she looked past his implacable expression, she saw something starved and feral lurking in his eyes. It was focused on her.

"What's wrong?" he asked.

"*What's wrong?*"

Lyla grabbed a two-thousand-dollar shoe and hurled it at him. He ducked to the side. The shoe whistled past and cartwheeled across the bedroom floor.

"What the fuck do you want from me, Gavin? Why am I here? I don't have anything else to give you!" She pounded her chest with a shaking fist. "I don't have anything left! Vengeance was more important to you than me, than your father, than *life*. You blamed me for Vinny's death, for *influencing* your choice. You threw me away like I always knew you would. I knew I would never be enough for you. You need the darkness. In that world you're judge, jury, and executioner. That's fine for you, but me? *No*."

She ran her hands through her tangled hair and paced in a small circle. After being chased, married, and brought back to her past life, she was beginning to unravel.

"I never wanted to be a part of your world. I know what I can handle, and what you do, I can't." Her chest burned as she glared at him through her tears. "Do you know what it feels like to be helpless? Like *really* helpless? I do."

Gavin reached for her, but she backed away, walking deeper into the closet filled with expensive clothes and sassy heels from another lifetime. Nothing mattered anymore. She didn't care what she looked like or what she wore. All that mattered was that she got through one day and then the next without giving in to the urge to slit her wrists.

How many times had she wondered if Carmen would be better off without her? The world wouldn't miss Lyla Dalton. She wasn't the CEO of a big corporation or an integral part of her family. Her parents barely noticed her existence, and she would be easily replaced at any job she qualified for. But she couldn't do that to Carmen. Her cousin had left everything for her. She suspected Carmen had needed the time-out as well. Now, life threw a curveball, and she was back with Gavin. Why? He didn't need her. She would rather live half a life where she had no feelings than a life with a man she couldn't trust and put her through hell. Again.

She couldn't look at Gavin and not think of his father. Manny and Gavin Pyre, the crime lords of Las Vegas, were the great loves of her life; the first people who saw something special in her. She would never know what drew her to these dangerous men, but they changed her life forever. Gavin Pyre was a law unto himself and would do whatever he thought was necessary. Case in point, she was back in Vegas with his ring on her finger.

"I can still hear your father screaming," she whispered and swallowed her own howl of grief. "I watched everything. I screamed until I had no voice."

"You have to know I would do anything in my power to take it back," Gavin said.

Lyla grasped handfuls of her hair. "I told you to stop, and you wouldn't!"

He said nothing. He just stood there like a gladiator from centuries past.

"What's the point?" she demanded, striding up to him and jabbing him in the chest. "Why make me your wife? Because that's what your father would have wanted?"

He shook his head.

"What, Gavin?" she shouted as she pounded his flesh with her fists. "You're not done with me yet? You want to punish me for Vinny's death? For not dying when I was stabbed? You can't hurt me more than I already do! I have nothing left!"

He wrapped her close. She scored his skin with her nails as she tried to get away.

"I'm not going to hurt you," Gavin said.

"Seeing you hurts me, having you touch me hurts," she sobbed. "*You* hurt me. You left me."

"I won't leave you again," he said into her hair, holding her desperately close.

"No! I'll never trust you or believe a word you say. I should have died that day with Manny."

Gavin jerked her chin up. "Don't say that."

She shoved at him and got nowhere. "What do you want from me?"

"We can make it, Lyla."

"I don't want to make it with you. You broke me!"

Gavin lifted her into his arms and hissed when she bit his shoulder. He cursed and carried her into the bathroom. When she tasted the unmistakeable tang of blood it shocked her so much that she didn't react when he began to undress her. It wasn't until her chest was bare and his hands stopped that she realized he was staring at her scarred abdomen. She whirled away and crossed her arms over her chest. White, raised scars and long gashes covered her body and made her look like Frankenstein. Even Carmen winced when she caught a glimpse of her disfigured body. She hadn't looked at herself in a mirror since the attack.

She couldn't stand the silence behind her. Of course, Gavin knew about her wounds, but seeing them was a different story. His body was a work of art, unblemished and powerful. Hers looked as battered as she felt. She would never be able to wear a dress or V-neck shirt without horrifying people. Her body was a walking testament to the evil that walked this earth.

"Get out," she whispered.

"Lyla—"

"Get *out*, Gavin!"

He hesitated before he walked out of the bathroom, quietly shutting the door behind him. She stripped off her remaining clothes and sank into the hot bath Gavin had prepared for her. When the wounds were fresh, the smallest droplet of hot water made her feel as if she was being stabbed again. Even now, she moved cautiously as the hot water touched her scars, but there was no pain. The sweet aroma of the bath salts and the size of the luxurious tub felt wrong after being on the road for so long. She stiffened when the door opened again.

"Clothes," he said and set something on the vanity before he left again.

She rested her forehead to her knees. Their talk wasn't over, not by a long shot, and she felt so incredibly weary. The tumult of events in the past few hours made her feel as if she'd aged ten years. She turned her back to the mirror as she dressed in the nightgown Gavin produced. It was cut low enough to show the beginning of the ragged scar between her breasts and the wound centimeters from her heart that should have killed her. She fussed with the nightgown before she brushed her hair. She wondered if there was a way to avoid Gavin and then scoffed. He refused to be left behind or ignored.

She walked into the bedroom and found Gavin sitting on the edge of the bed, waiting for her in sweatpants and nothing else. She wished he would wear a shirt but then realized she should be grateful he was wearing something. His eyes moved over her and then focused on her chest. Did her scars disgust him? Why the fuck did she care?

"I'm tired," she said.

Gavin's eyes flicked up to hers.

"I'll take one of the guest bedrooms." She started for the

door and was brought up short when he stepped in front of her.

"You sleep here."

"You're going to sleep somewhere else?" she asked pointedly.

"No."

"I'm not sleeping with you, Gavin."

"We're married."

"Don't you *dare* throw that in my face!" Lyla exploded, stomping her feet and waving her hands wildly. "We're as married as your father is alive."

Gavin rocked back as if she shoved him. "It's legal, Lyla."

"I'm not married until I feel married."

"We can rectify that."

She pointed her finger in his face. "Don't, Gavin."

"I'm not going to force you to have sex with me. I just need to be near you."

"Why?" she asked suspiciously.

He stared at her, his face a mixture of exasperation and anger. "I need to know you're with me." When she said nothing, his hands fisted at his sides. "I haven't had a decent night of sleep since Dad died. I need to hear you breathing. I need to touch you. Not sexually, if that's what you want."

"No sex," she growled and whirled away from him.

Out of habit, she took the side of the bed that faced the window. As she sank into the mattress, she suppressed a sigh of pleasure. It really was the little things in life...

Gavin climbed onto the opposite side of the bed. He didn't touch her, but she felt his body heat. How was she supposed to sleep beside her ex who was now her husband? Lyla stared blindly ahead for a long time before her eyes fluttered shut.

4

LYLA

LYLA OPENED her eyes and froze. She was lying on her side facing Gavin with her arm tossed over his middle, tucked against him as if they slept together every night. Apparently, her body forgot she wasn't with him anymore. Lyla spied the blue diamond ring on her finger and bared her teeth in a silent snarl. So what if she was 'technically' married to him. That didn't mean anything.

She took a minute to examine him. She had no idea what drove Gavin to do the things he did. He blamed her for Vinny's death, refused to leave the criminal world for her, and was an emotionless bastard when she woke in the hospital. Why look for her after he got out of jail? Why force her into marriage? Even though he denied it, she knew it had something to do with Manny. Maybe he felt guilty that she got hurt... No. If he felt guilty, he wouldn't have threatened to kill Carmen to get her to marry him. Seriously, Gavin was too complex to figure out, so she wouldn't.

Although he was asleep, his features weren't relaxed. He was tense as if he was ready to react at any second. Her hand twitched on his chest before she slowly began to pull away.

His eyes snapped open, and she stilled. Alert amber eyes moved over her face, and then he relaxed.

"Okay?" he asked.

He was asking if she was okay *now*? She needed him to ask that when she felt as if she died with his father. She needed him to ask that when he saw her in Montana. He didn't even ask how she was; he just demanded that she marry him.

Lyla pounded his chest with her fist and found small satisfaction in his grunt of surprise before she rolled out of bed and went into the bathroom. She locked the door and took care of business before she waltzed out. Gavin sat up in bed, and when she walked toward the door, he jumped up.

"Where are you going?"

"I'm hungry," she said shortly.

She was happy to see that Blade and the other security weren't patrolling the hallway. Having them hover after being on the road with Carmen would suffocate her. Dealing with Gavin was more than she wanted to handle. She opened the fridge, which was usually filled with pre-made meals, and wasn't disappointed. She made herself a bowl of yogurt, fruit, and granola and dug in. Gavin appeared as she finished. She ignored him and went back to the fridge. She popped some waffles in the toaster and slathered them with peanut butter and honey and felt semi-human again.

Gavin leaned against the counter with a cup of coffee and said nothing. She knew he was waiting for her to make the first move, which irritated the hell out of her. He pushed and shoved when he felt like it, and now he was acting like a patient gentleman, letting her set the pace of the morning.

"I want to talk to Carmen," she said.

Gavin waved a hand at the house phone. She ground her

teeth as she picked it up and dialed Carmen's prepaid number. Carmen picked up on the second ring.

"Lyla?"

"Yes. Are you okay?"

"Yes. You?"

She hesitated and then said, "Yes," a bit grudgingly.

"Really?" Carmen asked, obviously picking up on her tone.

"Yes." Aside from manhandling her and nearly punching Carmen, Gavin hadn't made any threatening moves toward her. The last time she arrived in Gavin's mansion, he'd roughed her up and scared the crap out of her. But she didn't sense rage in him this morning. Of course, that could change in a nanosecond. "Are you with your mom?"

"Yes. And he was telling the truth. My dad's gone."

Her heart clenched with regret and sadness. Uncle Louie, a former enforcer for Manny, was a good man who had been there for Lyla in her younger years. "When's the funeral?"

"In a couple of days."

Silence on both ends of the phone.

"Are you sure you're okay?" Carmen asked.

"Yes, I'll call you later. You're going to keep this phone?"

"Yes. You left yours behind, didn't you?"

"Yeah, but you can call me here."

"Okay. I love you. You need me, you call me."

"Same here. Love you. Bye."

Lyla hung up and turned to Gavin who hadn't moved. He looked dangerous and tempting. His wedding ring caught her eye.

"Your father's ring," she said and swallowed hard.

"Yes."

She took a deep breath, braced her feet apart, and looked him in the eye. "What am I doing here, Gavin?"

"I told you."

She glared at him. "You said you wanted everything I promised."

"Yes."

"There were conditions," she reminded him in case he forgot. "You broke your end of the deal."

"I did," he acknowledged.

"So you can renege on your end, and I *can't*? Fuck you, Gavin!"

"Vinny was murdered. What did you expect me to do?"

"I knew you would go after them." Why were they talking about this almost two years later? Oh, right. Because Gavin married her and wouldn't leave her alone. "I knew you would avenge Vinny, but you turned back into the man I ran from!" She tried to keep her voice even, but suppressed emotions were rising, refusing to be contained a second longer. "You blamed me for Vinny's death! Do you think I would have asked you to give up the title of crime lord if I knew Vinny would die?"

"It wasn't your fault. I apologize."

The calm delivery made her see red. She grabbed a mug and hurled it at his head. He sidestepped, and it smashed into the wall.

"You apologize? That's it? You think you can blame me for someone's death, apologize nearly two years later, and that'll make it okay? It doesn't work that way, Gavin!"

He took a sip of coffee, watching her with unreadable amber eyes.

"I don't want to be here," she said.

"I know."

"Yet you force me to be. Why? How many times do we have to do this before you realize this isn't going to work?"

"As many times as it takes. I fucked up. I might in the future, but I'll keep bringing you back. We're meant to be, Lyla."

She stared at him. "Are you crazy?"

"Some think so."

"I can't do this again," she whispered and was ashamed of her tears. She shook her head. "I can't."

"Lyla," he began and rounded the island.

"No!" she shouted and held her hand up like a traffic cop. "Just... no. I learn from my mistakes. I won't let you do this to me again."

"After Dad's murder..." He trailed off and set his coffee cup on the counter. His eyes never left hers as he crossed his arms over his chest. "I couldn't find out who was behind the attack. The trail was cold, and the cops knew something big went down. They were trying to get their hands on a body to pin me for first-degree murder, but they couldn't find one. They got me for money laundering instead. I let go of the underworld completely. I was going to tell you before I went to jail, but you were gone."

Lyla shook her head. "The damage is done, Gavin."

Gavin's muscles shifted as he tensed. "I know."

"You know? That's all you have to say?" she demanded, slapping her hands on the marble island. *They tortured him.*" She felt as if her heart were breaking all over again. "I watched them kill him." The awful memories, never far from the surface, made her body erupt with goose bumps.

"I'm sorry, Lyla."

"Don't say that to me! Don't you dare say that now!"

"What do you want me to say?"

"Nothing. Just like you did in the hospital."

His eyes had an unnatural sheen to them. "If I had known the price of avenging Vinny, I wouldn't have done it."

"But I told you what would happen. They won't stop even if you're out of the game." Something in his eyes told her that he agreed, but he didn't say it out loud. "What's done is done."

"Yes," he agreed. "I can't change our past, but I can damn well try to make it up to you."

"So that's why you brought me back? Because you feel guilty?" she asked in a dead voice.

"I feel guilty as hell." His eyes flicked to her chest and then back to her eyes. "You're mine to protect, and twice you were harmed. There won't be a third time."

"If you let me live my own life, there's no reason for them to come after me."

He said nothing for a beat and then, "I can't do that."

"Do what?"

"Let you live without me. I lashed out at you when Vinny died because I've never felt pain like that in my life. I knew he wasn't ready. *I* killed him, and I have to live with that. I also have to live with Dad's death." An agonized expression twisted his features. "I think about it every day, every hour. Knowing his killer is still out there..." The veins in his neck popped as he tried to rein in his rage. "I want—no, I *need* to kill him."

After what Lyla witnessed, she couldn't agree more. The man who killed Manny was a sadist. Because of him, she would never be the same.

"But I can't," Gavin said. "Maybe it's a good thing I went to jail. It forced me to stop obsessing, to think about my future..."

His unwavering stare made her heart skip with anxiety.

"You're my future," he said.

Lyla shook her head.

"You nearly died. You should have. Your injuries..." He shook himself as if he couldn't handle the images in his mind. "I never prayed in my life until that day, and I think God had mercy on me. I can live without my cousin, I can live without my dad, but I can't live without you."

The spark of warmth in her belly scared her. No. She couldn't let him in because he was a smooth talker.

"I know you hate me. You have every right to. I forced you into a life you didn't want. I'm selfish. And even if you can't forgive me, I don't want to live without you. I need you here." He ran his hands through his hair and paced away. He stood with his back to her as he admitted, "If I had an ounce of mercy in me, I'd let you live a normal life, but knowing you're out there means I can't leave you alone." He turned back to her, jaw tight, hands flexing at his sides. "I know you're angry, and that you'll never forget what happened. Neither will I. Make me pay for it."

"What?"

He spread his hands wide. "Do your worst, Lyla."

"You married me and brought me here to punish you?" He'd officially lost his mind.

"I brought you back because my life is worthless without you. I married you because I need you bound to me. You anchor me. After the hit on you and Dad, I lost it. I went on a fucking rampage. I killed..." He shook his head. "I need you to keep me from losing my shit. I need to see you, smell you, touch you. Your presence keeps me from going black."

"I can't do anything for you."

"You can. Yesterday with Carmen, I fucked up again. I can't rein it in. I'm a fucking bomb waiting to go off. That's why I took you in the room on the jet. You calm me the fuck

down. I can take anything if you're with me. I just...
need you."

Lyla didn't know what to say.

"I'm messed up," he said unapologetically, "and I don't
give a shit about most of the world, but you... you humanize
me. I need you with me, Lyla. I'll take whatever you
give me."

"I have nothing left to give," she whispered.

"Just you being here, it's enough."

She shook her head. "This is crazy."

"Yes."

"I can't—"

"You don't have to do anything."

"You really think that after all we've been through that
we can just go back to the way it was?"

"No. We'll never go back to that. We both have scars
from that day. We've both changed, but we're still us at the
core. I know what I need. What do you need, Lyla?"

"I need to be alone."

"Not going to allow that. What else?"

She wanted to throw something, but she was shaking
too badly to have decent aim. "I don't want drama."

"I'm planning to be pretty boring. I'm still CEO of Pyre
Casinos. I can do that job in my sleep. I gave up my title as
crime lord when I went to jail, and I haven't picked up the
mantle since I got out."

He looked as calm as could be, as if his psycho tackling
episode yesterday never happened. "You really are crazy."

He inclined his head. "I know."

"Who's the crime lord?"

"Don't know, don't care."

She didn't believe he was completely out of the underworld, but she didn't want to discuss it. "You forced me to marry you!"

"Yes."

"And now you expect me to sleep in the same bed as you, punish you, and live an ordinary life with you?"

"Is that a problem?"

"You're impossible! I don't want you, and I don't want to be here!"

"I know, but you aren't going anywhere."

"So I'm a captive again?"

"For now. For your own safety."

She wanted to rip her hair out. "I was fine on my own!"

"No, you weren't." He held up a hand when she would have raged at him. "Yesterday, your eyes were blank, your skin was pale, and you didn't eat. Today, you ate enough for the both of us, your cheeks are flushed, and you look like you might commit murder. You're waking up, Lyla. What you did this past year wasn't living."

"The last time I tried to live life to the fullest, I nearly died," she said bluntly.

"This time, you'll flourish."

"I don't believe it."

"You will in time."

"I hate you."

She stalked out of the kitchen and went upstairs. She couldn't bear to go back to the bed they slept in. The guest bedroom was clean and dusted. She flopped on the bed, folded her hands on her stomach and closed her eyes as a migraine snuck up on her. She breathed deeply and tried to organize her chaotic thoughts. When she felt the mattress dip, she shot up to a sitting position.

"What do you think you're doing?" she shouted.

"Lying down with you," Gavin said as he settled beside her.

"This is my space."

"Your space is my space."

"No, it isn't."

He didn't respond. He copied her, hands folded on his middle, and closed his eyes.

"Don't you need to go to work? You're the CEO."

"I'm on my honeymoon."

Lyla's head throbbed painfully. She dropped on the pillow and flung her arm over her eyes. "You're an asshole."

"Janice has been working overtime since news of Dad's murder hit the news and I went to jail. She's been waiting for something good to report. When I told her I was getting married, she nearly burst into tears."

"Who's Janice?"

"My PR person."

"And she thought after leaving you over a year ago that you'd be able to convince me to marry you?" she asked scathingly.

"She didn't ask, and I didn't tell her what I intended to do."

Lyla snorted. "Go away. You're giving me a migraine."

"I heard that sex cures headaches and migraines."

"You touch me, I'll murder you."

"Let me know if I can do anything to help," he said solicitously.

"Leaving me the fuck alone to live the life I choose would be nice."

"I can't do that. I haven't found a way to let you live without me. I don't intend to, either. Whatever you want to do, whatever you need, I'm here."

Lyla turned on her side away from him and tried to escape from his words.

———

Lyla woke in the afternoon and wasn't pleased to find Gavin still beside her. She ignored him as she slipped out of bed and went into the master bathroom to shower. She put on the most sexless pajamas in the closet and went to the kitchen where she warmed up spaghetti and meatballs. She sat on the counter and called Carmen who answered immediately and told her all was well on her end. Gavin entered the kitchen, freshly showered. Lyla tried to keep Carmen on the phone, but she had to attend to Aunt Isabel who Lyla could hear sobbing in the background. She reluctantly hung up and continued to ignore Gavin who warmed up his own meal and watched her in silence.

It didn't take more than ten minutes of his unwavering regard to make her retreat to the backyard. His presence roused too much inside her, and that was dangerous. She clung to the mundane because being in Gavin's vicinity, regardless of the fact he wasn't a crime lord anymore, wouldn't be an easy life. His adamant claim on her would flatter most women, but she was terrified. His love bordered on obsession. He would never let her go. She would never be free of Gavin Pyre, so what did that mean for her future?

The backyard was cast in orange light. Lyla sat on a lounge chair near the waterfall that cascaded into the Olympic sized pool and closed her eyes. She was so damn tired. It had been almost two years, and she hadn't recovered from Manny's murder. Gavin was right in one sense. The life she and Carmen indulged in wasn't living. It was existing. There was no joy or wonder in what they were doing. It was a tactic to avoid the real world. Gavin put a stop to that, and now he wanted to resume the life they would have had if Vinny and Manny hadn't been murdered. Was that even possible? Gavin was more volatile than ever, but he put a cap on it since they arrived in Vegas. He wasn't giving her the solitude she craved, but he also wasn't forcing his touch on her. He was hovering nearby, as if he really did need to be close to her. The fog of depression and hopelessness she existed in was beginning to lift.

She stiffened when the lounge chair beside her creaked. Freaking Gavin. She didn't have to open her eyes to confirm that he had, once again, interrupted her solitude. Her nose told her that he chose chicken Marsala for dinner. She wanted to ask him what he wanted from her, what he thought marrying her would accomplish, but she already knew the answer. He believed she could put his life on track to some kind of normal. How could she accomplish that when *she* didn't feel normal? She had been diced into pieces. Carmen attempted to glue her back together, but any moment now, she would fall apart again and she wasn't sure if Gavin could put her back together.

She let out a long breath and tried to ignore the tightness in her chest. Manny was the father she never had. He loved her unconditionally, as much as he had his own son. She would never be able to run to him for advice, never lay her head on his lap and have his hands sift through her hair. It was probably selfish of her to want him here for her sake. He was with his wife, the woman he loved more than life itself. He was in a better place, and they had to clean up their messy lives on their own. Manny had been able to slap sense into Gavin when he was going off the rails, but now that authority figure in their lives was gone forever. How did people go on after losing someone they loved?

"Dad left you half of his estate."

Her eyes popped open. "What?"

"You own a considerable chunk of Pyre Casinos."

Lyla didn't know how to process that and then narrowed her eyes. "And since you married me?"

"*We* own a considerable chunk of Pyre Casinos."

Lyla snorted. She didn't care about money or power, so it meant little to her, but the fact that Manny put her in his will made her heart ache.

"Dad left me his journals." Gavin ate slowly, staring out at nothing as he considered his words. "I've been reading them since I got out of jail. Some of the entries are revelations and thoughts, but a lot of them are addressed to me." He turned and looked at her. "He knew where you were the first time you left."

Manny had told her so, but she was wary of Gavin's reaction. Manny went so far as to give Gavin's investigator false leads to give her more time.

"He wrote a lot about you," Gavin said and shook his head. "Between the two of us, you never had a chance."

Her mouth curved the slightest bit. It was true. Manny hired her as an assistant within two weeks of meeting her. She worked with him after school and on weekends during her senior year. When she met Gavin, their chemistry had been undeniable. Gavin claimed her before she had a chance to go off to college and meet anyone else.

"He thought you possessed a part of my mom's spirit, and that's why we both fell hard for you."

The faint smile fell from her lips. She couldn't explain her connection to the Pyres. It was bizarre that she would have such a strong connection to people so different from her. They were the crime lords of Las Vegas and ran Pyre Casinos. She grew up in a middle-class family with a father who had a gambling addiction. They had nothing in common, yet she loved them beyond rational thought.

"Dad told you about it. You never said anything to me," Gavin said.

"It was between him and I."

"Maybe so, but you should have told me."

"That your father believed I had a piece of your mother's soul? Even *I* don't know how I feel about it."

"But you didn't push him away once you knew. It meant a lot to him."

She swallowed hard. "I know. He meant the world to me."

He touched her hair. The brush of his fingers was so light that she thought she imagined it at first. Then her hair shifted as he ran his fingers through the wavy mass. Her first instinct was to jerk away, but the motion reminded her so much of Manny that she stayed put.

"He wrote that he wanted to commit suicide before he met you. You gave him hope."

A tear trickled down her cheek. "Gavin, don't."

"You give me hope too."

"You both expected too much from me."

"I don't think so. You survived our worst. You're still you despite our influence. You're stronger than you think."

"I don't feel strong."

"Neither do I."

Lyla snorted. "But you are."

"There's strong and then there's strong," he said with a shrug. "You have inner strength. I don't. That's why you're able to live without me. I can't function not knowing where you are, without having you with me. I'm like my dad, I guess."

Lyla rested her cheek on her knees as she regarded him.

Gavin had a dominant, alpha personality. A keen business sense paired with lethal physical attributes ensured that no one fucked with him. His wealth gave him the power to do anything he wanted. To hear him admit that he wasn't strong was ludicrous. He could kill with his bare hands, and he thought of himself as weak?

"What else did you read?" she asked.

"He talked a lot about Mom. How he felt about her, how he suffered without her. He talked about life, and how I need to focus on you because you're all that matters."

"I figured he had something to do with this," Lyla said quietly and wriggled her left hand so the blue diamond shimmered.

"I had men looking for you before I cracked open his journal." Gavin paused while she digested that and continued, "What he wrote was confirmation for me. No matter what's happened in the past, we're supposed to be together. That's the only way we're both going to get through this life intact."

She wanted to argue, but she didn't have the energy. He continued to play with the ends of her hair as the sky darkened and night fell around them. The underwater lights from the pool illuminated their faces as they stared at one another.

"I fucked up with you so many times," Gavin said and stroked a gentle finger down her cheek. "Can you forgive me?"

"I don't know," she said honestly. "I don't blame you for going after Vinny's killers or even for blaming me for his death."

"Vinny's death is on me. I shouldn't have blamed it on you."

"Vinny's death is on the man who pulled the trigger,"

Lyla corrected, and when he looked like he wanted to interrupt, she lifted her finger. "Vinny accepted the position. You didn't force it on him, right?"

"No."

"Then let it go, Gavin."

"Have you?"

"After watching Carmen suffer every day, it's damn hard to convince myself all of this isn't my fault. She doesn't blame me, which makes me feel even worse. She doesn't blame you either."

Gavin didn't reply.

She looked away since it was easier to talk without staring into his dissecting gaze. While they were on the road, she wondered what she would say to him. Now that she had her opportunity, the words were lost in a maelstrom of emotion. He suffered because of Vinny and Manny's deaths. She could see that for herself. His need to be around her, to touch her was genuine. After everything, he needed comfort, but she wasn't sure she could give it to him. She was broken and bleeding herself. They were two broken and lost souls.

"Do you miss the dark stuff?" she asked.

"No."

"You haven't had to do anything for the criminal side of the business?"

"No. Everyone knows I'm out."

"But you still have Blade and the other security?"

"Dad and Vinny's killer is on the loose. I'm not taking chances."

"Are you hunting for him?"

"No trace of him. There's nothing to hunt."

"He might come for me to finish the job." She sensed his energy tinge the air with violence.

"I'd love to get my hands on him."

Lyla snatched her hair from his hands and got to her feet. She stood beside his lounge chair and glared down at him. "I'm not taking that chance again, Gavin! I won't!"

"I won't either." Gavin stared at her pensively. "Carmen taught you to shoot?"

"Yes. What does that have to do with anything?"

"It doesn't hurt to be prepared. Tomorrow we'll go to a shooting range, see how good of a shot you are."

"You're going to let me have a gun?"

"Whatever it takes for you to feel safe. I have guns stashed everywhere. I'll show you. You remember how to get out of the house if there's an attack?"

She nodded. He had a wine cellar with a secret door that led into the red mountains.

"I've added extra security measures. Blade will be with you at all times. I don't want you going anywhere without a security detail. I prefer you don't leave the house without me," he said.

Lyla didn't tell him that she didn't *want* to go anywhere without him. Despite the way she felt about Gavin, she knew he would die for her.

"That doesn't mean you're a prisoner. Our marriage is real; our life together is real. I want you to do what you want. If you want to go on a trip, I'll arrange time off from work. If you want to buy a new wardrobe or see your parents, you can. But Lyla..." He gave her a very direct and predatory look. "Don't run from me again. We can work this out."

"Work what out?" she snapped.

"Our relationship."

"We don't have a relationship."

"The ring on your finger says differently."

"Oh, this?" she asked sarcastically.

Gavin was off the lounge chair and in her face before she could pull the damn thing off her finger. He clasped her hand between his and dipped his head so their faces were less than six inches apart.

"Don't take it off."

His angry tone made her eyes narrow.

"You forced me to marry you."

"Yes, I did. You've taken off on me too many times. You need to get this, Lyla. You're stuck with me. Legally."

"I had my reasons for *taking off*." She yanked her hand from his. "You've hurt me more than anyone else. I don't know how I feel about you. Every instinct tells me I can't afford to be with you again. My heart can't take it. You flip flop between the ruthless crime lord and the man who says he can't live without me. Which man are you?"

"Both."

"That's what scares me," she said quietly. "You can't separate those men, and I never know when the other is going to take over."

"I'm not a crime lord any longer. The only man I am is the CEO of Pyre Casinos, but more importantly, I'm your husband."

She could feel his will pressing on her. It made her tip her chin up defiantly. She looked evil right in the eye. Gavin Pyre wouldn't intimidate her even if he was a murderer.

"Before Vinny died, you and I made promises to one another. I admit it. I lost it when he was murdered, and I took it out on you. I refused to leave the underworld after Vinny's death because it would make me look weak. I needed to put them in line. I thought they wouldn't retaliate, but it backfired. I left you in the hospital fighting for your life and unleashed hell in the underworld. I worked out my demons, but it wasn't enough. When I surfaced, the cops were waiting. Thank God my men are loyal to me. They covered my tracks. Not one crumb of evidence was found. You woke from your coma. I wasn't completely sane, so Blade sedated me so I could be calm enough to talk to you. That's why I was such a bastard that day. I focused on my objective and ignored what you went through because I couldn't handle it."

Gavin cupped the back of her neck and squeezed. When she tried to shrug off his hold, he pressed his lips against her temple.

"I need this," he whispered, and the pain in his voice made her freeze. "I've needed to say this for so long."

She closed her eyes as he cradled the back of her head. His other hand swept up and down her back as she trembled. His touch, his scent roused her emotions to a fevered pitch. She was torn between throwing herself into his arms or punching him in the face. Instead, she stood there with her eyes closed, trying to keep herself from reacting to anything he said.

"I can't begin to understand what you went through that day," he murmured, warm breath feathering over her face. "I don't blame you for running from me. I don't blame you for hating me. After I walked into the house and I saw you and Dad on the floor, covered in blood, not moving... I don't remember anything after that. I blocked it from my mind. You don't have that luxury. I'm so fucking sorry."

Her head dropped and landed on his shoulder. Tears slipped down her cheeks. She fisted her hands in his shirt to stop herself from screaming.

"I wasn't there for you when you needed me. I don't know what you went through. I can't imagine and I don't want to. I know the extent of Dad's injuries and yours." His hand swept over her as if reassuring himself that she was whole. "Your survival is a miracle, and I'm not going to waste it. Whatever you need, I'll give."

She couldn't hold back a keening sob. He wrapped her tight against him as she began to shake uncontrollably.

"I made promises to you that I've broken. I'm remaking them now. I love you. I want children with you. I want to spend the rest of my life with you." When she tried to push away, he made shushing sounds and rubbed her back soothingly. "I want to make you happy. I want you to teach me how to laugh again, how to feel without going off the deep end. I need you to let me take care of you. I need to see you heal, so I know I haven't destroyed the most important person in the world to me. I need you to give me hope."

She shook her head against his chest.

"I love you, Lyla. I'm fucked up, and you always seem to pay the price. Not this time. I'm out of the business and walking a straight line to you. Only you can get me through this. Blade's been sedating me since I got out of jail, so I stop breaking things... and people. I can act normal for a few hours at work before I have to leave or get sedated again. I need you to ground me. You don't need to love me back; you don't even need to like me. I just... need."

Lyla sniffled against his shirt. "I don't know if I can do this."

"You don't need to do anything. Just be with me."

She felt as if she hadn't slept in days. "I'm so tired."

Gavin didn't hesitate. He picked her up in his arms and carried her into the house. He took her upstairs to the master bedroom. She buried her face in the pillow and wept, great gasping sobs that racked her whole body. A warm, hard body wrapped around her.

"You're not alone," Gavin said into her hair. "I'm here. We're going to get through this."

5

GAVIN

GAVIN GRASPED Lyla's hand as they walked onto the gun range. Although she stiffened, she didn't jerk away. He held her while she cried her heart out last night. The sound of her sobs followed him into sleep. This morning, her eyes were swollen and lifeless, but she didn't protest when he asked if she wanted to go to the gun range. Now that she brought it up, he was eager for her to be armed and ready. It would make both of them feel better.

He had to admit that her wardrobe was lacking the necessary clothing for a visit to the range. She drew stares from men and women. She wore large sunglasses to cover bloodshot eyes, a sleeveless turtleneck, and short shorts with thigh-high gladiator sandals. It was warm out, so the turtleneck should be a last resort, but she didn't want to show her scars. The glimpse he had of her chest and abdomen had made him sick with rage. He had to resist the urge to pull her clothes aside so he could see everything. When she allowed him to touch her, he'd show her in no uncertain terms how he felt about her scars.

He stood back to watch her shoot and felt himself get

hard as she braced herself and took aim. Clearly, Carmen was a better marksman than he gave her credit for. Lyla had nearly perfect form, and her aim was better than he could have hoped.

"How did I do?" she asked when she took off her ear protectors.

"Excellent." He kissed her and ignored her startled expression. He wouldn't stop pushing until she was completely his... and maybe not even then. "I'm going to have Blade bring you to the range a couple of times a week to keep you fresh. He can even teach you to spar if you feel up to it."

Lyla nodded. He put his arm around her and stared down a guy who was gawking at her. She was oblivious to the attention, which is the only reason he was able to keep his shit together. If she ever looked at another man, he wasn't sure what he would do. Just the thought of that geeky IT guy made him want to kill. It crossed his mind when she went on the run that she might have gone back to him. If he wasn't so pissed at Carmen, he would have thanked her for keeping Lyla away from that bastard.

He helped her into the back of the SUV and didn't apologize when he rested his hand on her thigh. She tried to shift away, but he tightened his hold. When she glared at him, he held her gaze with a deadpan one. He didn't lie or exaggerate. He needed touch to anchor him. Blade had a syringe filled with a sedative just in case he went off the rails. If he didn't have so much respect for his second in command, he would have shot Blade the first time he was drugged.

"Where are we going?" she asked.

"We're going to get you new clothes, and then we'll get you a gun."

"I don't need new clothes."

"If you want to go to the gun range, I think you need jeans and sneakers, not heels."

Lyla made a face. He resisted the urge to stroke her thigh. That would be pushing it. Touching her at all was pushing it, but he couldn't help it. He wanted to think he made progress with her last night. Mere words wouldn't make everything okay, but they didn't hurt. He would do everything in his power to make her happy.

When they arrived at the mall, Blade and the other men fanned out so they didn't look so obvious. When he paused by the directory, unsure where to go, Lyla sighed and tugged him in the direction of a boutique. When a bubbly sales associate approached her, he relaxed. He wanted Lyla to feel comfortable. If her existing wardrobe didn't work, they would throw it away and start over.

He stopped the sales associate as she bustled around. "She needs everything—shoes, underwear, jeans, skirts, dresses, the works."

She looked him up and down and winked. "You got it, big boy."

Gavin snorted as the sales associate walked away.

Blade came up beside him. "All good?"

He ran a hand through his hair. No. It wasn't 'all good.' It may *never* be 'all good,' but he could hope. "As good as can be under the circumstances."

"You're keeping your shit together."

"She lets me touch her. That's enough for now," he said and started forward when he lost track of her. "Where is she?"

"Dressing room," Blade said calmly.

He tried to ignore the anxiety as he checked his phone and replied to Marcus, the new COO of Pyre Casinos.

Marcus was a young, intelligent bastard who kept things running better than he and Vinny ever had. He appointed Marcus right before he went to jail. Marcus could have taken advantage of his absence, but instead maintained everything to perfection. Upon his release, Marcus began to suggest plans to expand the Pyre Empire. Occupied with Lyla and keeping his mind off a murderous rampage, he was grateful for Marcus's eagerness to take on the bulk of his workload. Marcus had been on the periphery of Gavin's mind since he became an intern at Pyre Casinos. Marcus didn't have a privileged background, and his hunger to prove himself honed a keen business sense that Gavin used to his advantage.

When he couldn't stand it any longer, he went into the dressing room, which had five rooms and three large mirrors against one wall. Only one door was closed.

"Lyla?" he called.

"Yes?"

He rubbed a hand over his sweaty face and hid shaking hands in his pockets. He had to keep it together. "Are you finding what you need?" he asked lamely.

A pause and then, "Yes."

Feeling like an idiot, he sat because his legs were weak. He couldn't stand being away from her. He had her back for two fucking days. His worry was justified, wasn't it? She had been butchered and then disappeared for a year and a half. That wannabe fucking crime lord was still breathing, and Lyla didn't want to be here. Of course, he was on edge. It would take time for them to trust one another, and he wouldn't take chances with her.

The sales associate came in with armfuls of clothes and paused when she saw him.

"Miss me?" she asked cheekily.

"Missed my wife," Gavin said and jerked his head at the closed door.

"Aw! Honey, this man is a keeper!"

Lyla gave him an unreadable look when she opened the door. The sales associate bustled in and went into great detail about the dresses and outfits.

"I don't want anything low cut," Lyla said, voice quiet but firm.

"No?" the sales associate asked, bewildered. "Your body is banging."

"I have," Lyla paused and glanced at Gavin before she finished, "a lot of scars on my chest."

The sales associate looked startled and then sympathetic. "Okay. Well, let me see what else I can find." She grabbed more than half of the outfits and left.

Lyla and Gavin stared at one another. He wanted to go to her but knew this wasn't the time or place.

"You can model for me if you want," he said, trying to sound upbeat even as a bubble of rage began to creep up his throat. When he found the fucking coward who attacked his father and Lyla, he would make them suffer a thousand times over for what they did to his family.

Lyla bared her teeth and closed the door in his face. He relaxed on the sofa and answered emails and returned some phone calls while the sales associate ran in and out of the dressing room with clothes. Lyla didn't model anything for him, but he was satisfied that she wasn't throwing a fit over his hovering.

They went to three more stores. It amused him that, unlike her old wardrobe, she was going for comfort rather than fashion. She did accept several dresses, but her choices were practical and not aimed toward seduction. He didn't bother to tell her it didn't matter what she wore. He was painfully aroused whether she wore lingerie or sweatpants. Although his eyes moved over her body often, he was drawn to her face. The way her eyes lit up when she liked something, her pursed lips when she was making a decision, and the smile that didn't come often enough. He was to blame for that.

Blade and the men were relieved to make their way out of the mall and perked up when they went to a gun shop. Lyla didn't go for something girly and cute. She chose a stainless steel semi-automatic pistol that was light, small, and powerful. He approved and watched as she tried out her choice in the store's gun range. After unloading the bullets into a target, she turned to him and nodded. Lyla had changed since Dad's death. She had become solemn and wary, but he believed her light was still there, just buried. He kissed her on the lips and took care of the purchase.

When they got back to the car, he gave directions to a trusted establishment. He put his arm around Lyla as they walked into the restaurant. The hostess recognized him and directed Blade and the guys to two tables that flanked the one he and Lyla sat at. Before they opened their menus, the owner appeared in a chef's outfit. Gavin rose and hugged him.

"Gavin, you good?" Carlo asked.

He nodded and gestured to Lyla. "This is my wife, Lyla."

Lyla rose and Carlo engulfed her in a hug. Gavin would have been jealous to see her in another man's arms if it wasn't for her startled expression.

"I wasn't invited to the wedding?" Carlo demanded.

"Shotgun wedding," Gavin said.

Carlo winked at Lyla. "I understand. I had to get my woman pregnant before she'd marry me."

Lyla's eyes bugged. Carlo sobered and regarded both of them solemnly.

"My condolences about Manny," Carlo said. "He was a good man."

Gavin's stomach tightened with his constant companion, rage. "He was."

"Did you catch the bastard who did it?"

It burned him to say, "Not yet."

Carlo looked at Lyla, and his face softened. "The Pyres are good people, which makes you good people. We protect our own."

Lyla nodded but shot Gavin a puzzled look before Carlo clapped his hands together.

"I will send you amazing dishes. Just you wait," Carlo declared and noticed Blade and the others. "I will send *lots* of amazing dishes. I'll get to it."

Carlo disappeared into the kitchen as quickly as he appeared. Lyla sat and raised her brows. He enjoyed seeing her curiosity. Every day she seemed a little more animated and a little less like a woman who had survived hell.

"Dad helped Carlo's family open this restaurant. They've done well and expanded to other cities," Gavin said.

A server appeared with champagne bottles and poured glasses for all three tables. Lyla sipped and nodded, clearly pleased with the taste.

"Did he really get his girlfriend pregnant so she would marry him?"

Gavin's lips twitched. "Yes."

"Why wouldn't she marry him?"

"She doesn't believe in marriage. Hardcore feminist."

"Why did getting pregnant change anything?"

"When she had the baby, her feminist ways went out the window. She demanded his help because she couldn't do it on her own, but Carlo wouldn't unless she married him." He chuckled at Lyla's dumbfounded expression. "And they lived happily ever after. Carlo has five kids. His wife is extremely trapped."

"He did it purposely?"

Gavin didn't answer, which made her snort. When a plate of appetizers appeared, he felt a flood of warmth when she reached for it without waiting for him. She was hungry. Good. She ate most of the dish before realizing he hadn't eaten a thing.

"Try it. It's great," she said and moved the plate toward him.

He took one to appease her before he pushed it back. He chewed and didn't taste anything. "Finish it."

Lyla shrugged and cleaned up the first appetizer as two more were brought to their table. She didn't try to initiate conversation, which never bothered him before, but now he was unsure of her. He didn't know what she was thinking or feeling. Lyla was an introvert and all in her head, which scared the crap out of him.

"You liked being on the road?" he asked because he needed to know.

Ice blue eyes clashed with his. His belly clenched. That face. That was all it took for him to fall for her. Lyla was innocent but confident enough to challenge him from the beginning. She knew her worth and left when she caught him cheating on her. She didn't care about money or status, which made her the best and worst because he couldn't bribe her. Nothing mattered except who he was as a person, and most of the time, he didn't like the reflection of himself in her eyes.

"Being on the road gave us both the escape we needed," Lyla said.

Even though he didn't like it, he understood. "You didn't have any trouble on the road?"

"We had trouble with some truck drivers at a pit stop, but Carmen pulled out her gun and that put an end to it. That's when she taught me how to shoot. We had a bear visit us once when we were asleep. He rocked the RV. That was interesting." Lyla finished her first glass of champagne and gave the server a small nod of thanks when it was refilled. "We broke down on the freeway once."

"What happened?"

"Flat tire." She gave him an unreadable look. "Do you know how eager men are to help a couple of blondes in short shorts?"

His hands fisted. He could damn well imagine men pulling on the side of the road to help Lyla and Carmen. Both of them were stunning. Together, they were trouble. Lyla was ice; Carmen was fire. They were opposites that complemented one another. He had been jealous of their close bond on more than one occasion, but having Carmen take Lyla from him when he didn't know the location of his father's killer made her an enemy in his book. Lyla watched him steadily. She knew he was a jealous, possessive bastard. Was she teasing or punishing him?

"We handled life on the road rather well," she finished.

He didn't like that answer. He didn't want her to be able to live without him, and she knew it. "Well, now you can have a normal life."

"Normal?" she echoed as if she didn't know the definition of the word.

He didn't blame her. His life was anything but normal and because of him, hers went haywire. "Well, *our* kind of normal. As mundane as you want it to be."

The main course of perfectly prepared steaks was placed

in front of them. Once again, he felt a hum of pleasure as Lyla cut into hers with gusto.

"How are my parents?" she asked without looking at him.

"Still receiving the allowance you granted them." He hesitated and then said, "It's very modest."

"Even when my dad was making good money, my mom cut coupons. Plus, my dad doesn't need extra money to gamble. I know exactly how much they need to survive." She looked up from her steak. "And my father doesn't deserve even that. Thank you."

"My pleasure." And it was. He couldn't care less about Lyla's father, but whatever made him look less like a monster, he would do. Gladly. "Do you want to see them?" He knew for a fact that Lyla hadn't contacted her parents. He monitored them closely and discovered they were just as clueless to Lyla's whereabouts. Like his father, Gavin couldn't believe how little Lyla's parents cared for their only child.

"I expect I'll see them at the funeral since Mom is Aunt Isabel's cousin," Lyla said.

He didn't want her near Carmen, but he wouldn't stop her from attending her uncle's funeral. "When is it?"

"Day after tomorrow. Starts at noon and then there's a get-together at Carmen's mom's house afterward."

"I'll go with you."

She didn't argue. The steak nearly melted on his tongue. They ate in silence. When she finished, she sat back and folded her hands over her stomach.

"I need a nap," she said.

She was sleeping a lot. Not that he minded since he had become an insomniac. Having her home allowed him to sleep longer than three hours at a stretch.

He signaled to Blade before he grabbed Lyla's hand. They went into the kitchen to thank Carlo and say goodbye. It was late afternoon when they drove home. Lyla staggered into the house and collapsed on the couch. When Gavin offered to carry her upstairs, she gave him a long look and turned on the TV. She stretched out on the sofa and cuddled into a pillow as she flipped through the channels. Blade and the guys dropped her shopping bags in the foyer. The maid would put her clothes away tomorrow.

Gavin settled on the sofa and watched her out of the corner of his eye. She didn't look as if she wanted to bolt, but then again, he wasn't the best at reading her. He retrieved his laptop and worked while she relaxed and eventually drifted to sleep.

He wanted to touch and stroke her, but he wouldn't jeopardize any progress he made. He wanted her more than anything in the world, but he couldn't rush this. He had to be patient, a virtue he didn't possess. At least she was here with him. In Montana, he had bullied and coerced her. Now, he would woo his wife into spending a lifetime with him and giving him all the things he needed from her. If she knew the depth of his obsession, she would run, so he had to keep it in check. Lyla already thought the worst of him, and he gave her good cause. What good he possessed, he hoped it would be enough for Lyla to stay with him because he wasn't capable of letting her go.

6

LYLA

THEY PULLED up to a humble church bursting at the seams with people. Lyla wore a new sleeveless dress with a high neck collar and black pumps. She was glad Gavin had insisted on a new wardrobe, though she would never tell him so. Her old wardrobe was for arm candy—a woman who showed off her assets at every opportunity and didn't have a care in the world. Lyla felt decades older than the woman who wore expensive labels with such carelessness.

She wasn't surprised when Gavin grabbed her hand as they walked toward the church. Over the past two days, Gavin was never far away. She would have called it stalking if she didn't see that the only time he was completely relaxed was when he was touching her. They slept in the same bed, and although she always fell asleep without touching him, she woke in his arms. Neither of them said much. She mulled over the things he said and gauged his actions. He seemed content to work on his laptop and be as close as possible without making any sexual moves, which made her feel safe yet frustrated. She wasn't ready even though her body had a different opinion. She couldn't deny that his constant presence and touch affected her. When he came for her in Montana, he had been the merciless crime lord. Since they had arrived in Las Vegas, he changed. He was affectionate, honest, considerate, and eager to please. He was the Gavin she always knew he could be.

Over the past couple of days, she realized one thing. He took their marriage seriously, never mind that he forced her into it. There was no out this time. Gavin wouldn't allow it. She had no idea what he envisioned for their future, but he was determined to make this work.

When they entered the church, people turned to look at their entourage and quickly averted their eyes when they recognized Gavin. The chatter dimmed and people made way for them. It never occurred to her to wonder what the media reported. The facts were that Gavin went to jail for money laundering and both Vinny and Manny were murdered. She had no clue if her injuries had been reported or what her parents had been told. She spotted her mother standing with Carmen and Aunt Isabel. Mom rushed forward and gave her a tight hug. Lyla felt absolutely nothing. She was aware that Gavin hadn't released her. Mom drew back and gave Gavin an overly bright smile.

"I heard you got married!" Mom said.

"Yes." Gavin didn't elaborate.

"Finally," Mom said playfully and held up Lyla's left hand to examine the ring. Her mouth fell open. "It's gorgeous!"

"I want to give my condolences to Aunt Isabel," Lyla said, aware that all eyes were on them, and her mother was making a scene.

"Oh, of course, dear," Mom chirped.

Her mother didn't ask where she'd been for the past year and a half or if she was happily married. Her mother only saw what she wanted to because she lived off Gavin's good will. Lyla tried to brush away her bitchy thoughts as she hugged Aunt Isabel who looked skeletal and wan. Aunt Isabel and Carmen stood side by side. The last time she'd been in this church was for Vinny's funeral. Mother and daughter were widows long before they should have been. Gavin released her so she could embrace her aunt who was trembling and barely keeping it together.

"He was a good man," Lyla whispered in her ear. Uncle Louie was a superb uncle. She had fond memories of sleepovers at their house. Aunt Isabel and Uncle Louie were down to earth, practical, and loving. Her heart ached for simpler times.

"He was." Aunt Isabel cupped her chin and gave her a watery smile. "He loved you and Carmen so much."

Lyla blinked back tears. So much loss in so little time. She released Aunt Isabel and hugged Carmen who sagged against her.

"Are you okay?" Carmen whispered in her ear.

"Yes. Are you?"

"I'm going to be glad when this is over. You're coming to the house after, right?"

Lyla nodded and kissed her cheek. "I'll save you a seat."

Lyla turned, surprised to see that Gavin had Aunt Isabel's hand clasped in both of his. Her aunt looked a bit shell-shocked, but she nodded as he spoke.

"Thank you so much," Aunt Isabel said.

Gavin turned, and though his eyes hardened when they landed on Carmen, he inclined his head respectfully. "I'm sorry for your loss."

Carmen said nothing. Gavin followed Lyla to the front pew while Blade and the other guards stood on the sidelines, guarding the exits. They didn't stand out as much in this crowd since their black suits blended in with the other attendees. Lyla spotted her father before she took her seat. The last time she saw him, he had been bedridden from Gavin's beating. She hoped he wasn't stupid enough to say or do anything today. Gavin wouldn't stand for it and neither would she. Watching a sadist beat Manny to death changed her. Manny had been her father in every way but blood. She was honored to have him in her life and wouldn't take any bullshit from her biological father. Not anymore.

Gavin sat on her left. He placed his arm on the back of the pew and drew her against him. "You okay?"

She let out a shuddering breath. "I don't think I can take another funeral."

His hand clamped around the back of her neck and squeezed.

She looked up at him. "What did you do about your dad?"

His jaw clenched. She felt awful for bringing it up, but she had to know.

"He didn't have a funeral. I couldn't with his killer on the loose. His ashes are at the house."

"They are? Where?"

"In my office." His eyes raked her face. "Is that fucked up?"

She shook her head. "No. I'm glad he's still with us."

She thought she saw a glimmer of wetness in his eyes before he leaned down and kissed her. It was a soft, gentle kiss and over with before she could react.

Carmen sat on her right as the pastor took the stage. Carmen took Lyla's hand as people took the stage to share memories and stories. Lyla laughed and cried with the congregation.

"I have to go up. Will you come with me?" Carmen whispered.

Lyla hesitated for a moment and then said, "Of course."

They rose, hand in hand, and walked to the podium. Lyla felt clammy and cold as she looked out over the church. They had been anonymous wanderers for over a year. If it weren't for Carmen, she would have walked off the stage. Would they see beneath the carefully applied makeup to the broken being she was inside?

Carmen's stifled sob got Lyla's attention. Carmen gave her a pleading look. Her cousin had done so much for her. Now, it was time to forget her personal shit and step up. Lyla approached the mic. Her eyes fell on Gavin in the front row, watching her with steady amber eyes. The force of his personality made most people edge away, but she absorbed his strength.

"Uncle Louie was a great man," she said and was proud that her voice didn't shake. "He convinced my parents to leave California and come to Sin City where he guaranteed that we'd fit in."

Carmen let out a broken laugh, and Lyla managed a small smile.

"He was right." Lyla's eyes moved to her parents and then to Aunt Isabel who had a hand over her mouth as she wept. "He welcomed me in as if I was his daughter and made Vegas feel like home. I'll never forget him." Another father figure lost. A lance of pain struck her heart, and she wanted to cry and rage. "He raised one of the best women in the world." Lyla raised Carmen's hand in hers. "My cousin lost her father and husband, but she's still here."

A smattering of claps filled the church.

"Our lives are better because he was in it. That's how we go on, by remembering the good times."

Aunt Isabel gave her a watery smile and nodded. Lyla stepped back, and Carmen took the mic. Her voice was shaky but strong.

"My father was a good man. He taught me to love with all my heart and to support and protect our family." Carmen looked at her mother. "We're going to get through this, Mom. Thank you all so much for coming here today to celebrate his life with us. He's in a better place now. That's what matters."

Hums of agreement rang through the church as they took their seats. Carmen's uncle closed the funeral with an acoustic guitar playing in the background. Carmen and Lyla sat with their hands clasped to comfort one another. They said death came in threes. Lyla closed her eyes and prayed this would be the last one for a long time. She wouldn't be able to handle the death of another person so close to her.

"I'll see you at the house," Carmen said when they rose at the end.

Lyla kissed her cheek and nodded. Gavin pulled her out of a side door. Blade pulled the SUV around, and they were off before anyone could waylay them.

"That was a good speech," Gavin said, squeezing her hand.

She let out a long breath. "He was a great guy."

"He was. He liked Vinny."

"Yes. What did you say to Aunt Isabel?"

"I'll cover the cost of the funeral and whatever else she needs help with."

"What?"

Gavin glanced at her. "She's family."

"My family," Lyla corrected.

"She's Vinny's mother-in-law. He isn't here to help, but I am."

Family loyalty. His generosity surprised and touched her. Who was this man?

They reached the house as Carmen and her mother pulled up. Carmen gave Gavin a frosty look before they went inside and prepared for their guests. Gavin and the men stayed out of the way as Carmen talked to the caterer. Lyla reluctantly acted as hostess and greeted people at the door before ushering them into the backyard where everything was set up. Lyla recognized some of her family from her mother's side. No one asked about her life with Gavin. Everyone knew he had been in the press on suspicion of murder and criminal activity. They seemed to realize it was best they didn't know.

Seeing familiar faces should make her feel warm and fuzzy inside, but she felt anxious and weary instead. Making polite chitchat was something she used to do so effortlessly, but now, she wanted to go into a dark room and shut the door. Smiling took more effort than it should, and she had a raging headache. After mingling for an hour, she made her way to the house for solitude and came face to face with her father.

"You got nothing to say to me?" Pat asked.

Lyla crossed her arms over her chest. "Am I supposed to go out of my way to say hi to you?"

Her tone, derisive and sharp, caught him off guard. She'd never spoken to him like this in her life, and it felt damn good. He always treated her like dirt, but no longer. She sacrificed herself to save his ass after he stole half a million from Gavin. Her father's gambling addiction made him reckless and stupid. Gavin had every right to end her father's life for embezzling, yet Gavin let him get away with it because she came back to him. Her father's punishment was broken bones, a tap on the cheek for his sins. Now,

Gavin paid his bills since no one would hire an accountant with a tarnished reputation. Her parents didn't ask about her well-being, the rumors swirling about Manny's death, or her disappearance. All he thought about was himself. Typical.

"You can't talk to me like that," he snapped.

"I can talk to you however I want," she said crisply. "What do you want?"

"We have to talk."

"About what?" she asked suspiciously.

"That shit allowance you have us on. It's too small."

Of course, he wanted to discuss money. That's the only reason he bothered to talk to her. When he had a string of bad luck in her senior year and couldn't pay the mortgage, she started working for Pyre Casinos, which is where Manny came in. He and Gavin had been there for her ever since. When she began to date Gavin, he gave her an allowance that she used to help her parents pay their bills when they came up short. Gavin was still paying their bills, and her greedy father wasn't satisfied.

"You shouldn't have an allowance at all," Lyla said and turned away.

He whirled her back to face him. "Don't talk to me like that, you bitch."

She wrenched her arm out of his hold. When he reached for her again, she knocked his hand away. Her hand tingled from the impact, but she didn't shake away the pain. She endured mindless agony when she was carved open. This was nothing. She looked death in the eyes and lived to tell the tale. She faced off with her father and sensed someone approach. She had no doubt who it was when she felt the force of his fury.

"Don't touch me," Lyla hissed at Pat.

"I need more money."

Gavin gripped her waist and squeezed. Her father took a step back, and his righteous fury dialed down a bit, but it was still evident.

"I need more," her father said again.

"For what?" Lyla asked, already knowing but wanting to hear whatever bullshit answer he came up with this time.

"The bills are going up," he said lamely.

"Maybe you should downsize and move into an apartment," Lyla suggested.

Pat's eyes flicked to her ring. "You're swimming in money and can't give your father a couple of extra thousand? You worthless whore."

Gavin lunged, but Lyla stepped in front of him so he couldn't get at her father. Gavin tried to push her to the side, but she clung to him and he stopped.

"You just lost your allowance," she said and Gavin stilled.

"What?" her father shouted.

"You stole half a million and gambled it away. Then Gavin gives you an allowance to survive, and you're still not satisfied. You insult me and treat me like I'm nothing. Well, from now on, we are nothing. You never acted like a father, so my duty is done. Find a way to get a job and survive. If Mom needs a place to stay, she has one. You? No. I'm done."

Lyla pushed against Gavin, and he went willingly as they walked away from her father. Of course, their argument had attracted some attention, but once she made eye contact, people turned away and resumed talking.

"I'm your father!" Pat shouted.

Lyla closed her eyes at her father's furious bellow. He was a glutton for punishment. Gavin's body was tight against hers. She knew he wanted to pummel her father, or worse.

Lyla took a deep breath and turned to her father who was red in the face and dripping with sweat as if he'd run a marathon.

"You're not my father. My father was murdered nearly two years ago," Lyla said loud enough for everyone to hear.

Gavin's arm around her flexed.

"Manny Pyre?" Her father scoffed. "He got what he deserved."

Lyla wasn't aware that she moved. One moment, she was staring at him with a good ten feet between them, and the next, she was in his face. Her fist flashed out and rammed into his mouth. He stumbled back and fell to the ground, cursing. Lyla stood over him with her fists clenched, shaking like crazy.

"Don't you ever talk about Manny like that!" she raged.

"Did you fuck father and son?" her father jeered.

Lyla dropped on top of her father, used one hand to grab a fistful of his shirt and used the other to belt him across the face. There was a sickening crack as his nose broke and blood dribbled down his face.

"Both of them are better men than you will ever be. They would do anything for me. What have you *ever* done except cause me grief? You care about no one but yourself," Lyla screamed and drew her fist back again. Before she could land the hit, she was lifted off her father. Even as Gavin carried her away, she kicked and caught Pat on the temple. "If I *ever* hear you insult my family again, you'd better hope I'm not armed, you son of a bitch! You're lucky I didn't let them finish you off, you worthless piece of crap!"

Lyla cursed as Gavin walked through the house. She didn't stop shouting until she was tossed into the back of an SUV and pinned to the seat.

"Holy fuck!" Gavin tucked his head under her chin and began to laugh.

"That was amazing," Blade said as the SUV pulled away from the curb.

"Why did you stop me?" Lyla screamed and bucked beneath Gavin, bloodlust clouding all rational thought. "I sacrificed *everything* for him! I could rip him apart. Why didn't you kill him when you had the chance? If I ever see him again, I—*Why the fuck are you laughing?*"

"Oh, baby, that just made my day," Gavin said breathlessly and raised his head. He had a broad grin on his face, and his eyes were shining with delight. "I enjoyed beating his ass, but watching you do it was ten times better. Then you jumped on him and kept going."

He leaned down and kissed her. Rage morphed into something carnal as his tongue slipped into her mouth. Lyla's fingers dug into the back of his suit and her legs wrapped around him. Gavin sensed the change. The kiss became deeper and more seductive. His tongue stroked hers while one of his hands began to knead her breast. Lyla bit his lip and wrenched her mouth away.

She looked toward Blade and the guard riding shotgun. The radio was blasting and they both stared straight ahead. Gavin gripped her chin and turned her face back to him.

"You want me?" he asked in a low, growly voice that made her instantly wet. When she hesitated, his hold tightened fractionally. "Do you?"

"Have I ever stopped?" she snapped.

Gavin was selfish and possessed a code that would make most people cringe, but he loved her. She was so fucking tired of feeling dead inside, of wondering what her fate was. She was tired of being a means to an end. Gavin looked at her as if she meant everything in the world, and it beckoned her out of the darkness into the light. No matter how much she wanted to suppress her emotions, they were at full mast right now.

Gavin folded one of the seats down. She stared, bemused, as he crawled in the back of the SUV and beckoned. His eyes were blind with need. He didn't give a fuck, and at the moment, neither did she. Lyla crawled into the back, and he flipped the seat up. He dragged her beneath him and ran his hand up her thigh before slipping his fingers beneath her underwear. She let her legs fall open. He hissed when his fingers slipped easily into her. She was soaked. She wasn't sure if it was the adrenaline or because it was Gavin. Death pressed in around them. She needed affirmation that she was alive and that someone would care if she was gone.

She reached for his zipper and jerked it down. He was going commando. His fully erect cock fell into her hand. She gripped and gave him one long stroke. He jerked her hand away and positioned himself between her legs.

"I'm not going to last. It's been too fucking long," he said through clenched teeth.

He latched his mouth on hers and entered her with a hard thrust, going in to the hilt. She gasped and dug her fingers into his suit as he ground himself against her. There was no give on the floor. She moaned into his mouth as the radio, playing hard rock, blasted even louder. Gavin delved both hands into her hair as he pounded into her. She wrapped her legs around his waist and sent her hands questing over him, seeking skin. She yanked his shirt from his slacks, shoved her hands beneath the fabric and dug her nails into his muscled back. Gavin sped up his thrusts. Her eyes flew open as she climaxed, breaking their kiss to bury her face in his chest as her body convulsed.

"Look at me," Gavin commanded.

She opened blurry eyes and saw Gavin above her, face drawn with unquenchable hunger. She was dimly aware of the car rocking from side to side as Blade made turns. She glimpsed buildings through the long windows on either side of them.

"I love you," he said.

"I know," she said and bucked as he planted himself deep.

"I'll love you till the day I die."

She dragged his mouth to hers for a desperate kiss, hands claiming as much of him as she could reach. Gavin shuddered and braced his hands on either side of her as he rushed toward climax. She watched his eyes burn to gold as he flooded her with his seed. He kept thrusting until he had nothing left and then collapsed on top of her. Lyla wrapped her arms around him, panting.

"I won't fuck up this time," Gavin said against her ear.

"Shh." She cradled his face and kissed him.

He moaned into her mouth and kissed her back. Her body buzzed with adrenaline and endorphins. He rolled until she was splayed over him. She braced her hands on either side of his head and rocked her hips. He hissed and spanned her waist with both hands.

Lyla sat up and realized they were on the freeway. There were cars on either side of them and if the windows weren't tinted, some of the truck drivers would have seen a show. Instead, the only ones who knew what was going on were the two other men in the car. Blade had his shades on, so she wasn't sure if he was staring at her in the rearview mirror or straight ahead. She moved on Gavin and was urged onward by the adoration on his face. He quickly grew hard again, more than ready to meet her needs. He was completely open to her, his emotions on full display, and it spurred her on. His hands flexed on her as she bounced and then tipped forward, hands braced on either side of his head as he thrust upwards.

"Fuck!" she shouted as he reared up and latched onto her neck.

He fucked her like a demon. She collapsed on top of him, clutching his head to her when she came.

His teeth sank into her neck as he climaxed. She knew she would bear his mark and didn't care. She lay boneless on him until the music quieted.

"We're almost there, boss," Blade called.

Gavin lapped at her neck. "You okay?"

"Mmm." The part of her that cared what others thought urged her to make herself presentable, but a greater part of her didn't care. It didn't matter how others perceived them. She had to live in the moment and embrace her feelings. That was what made her human.

"If Blade saw anything, I'll kill him," Gavin said against her neck.

Lyla laughed.

"It's not funny," he growled.

Gavin looked ravished, delectable, and dangerous.

"Maybe if we didn't fuck in a car with him, then he wouldn't see anything," she said and brushed kisses over his face.

Gavin closed his eyes and rocked his hips. His cock twitched to life.

"We're almost home," she said and toppled to the side with a loud thump. She giggled as Gavin forced himself into his pants. She felt blissfully unconcerned as they pulled up in front of the mansion, and Gavin fussed with her clothes. Blade stopped the car and flipped up the back door of the

SUV to let them out. Gavin hopped out and hauled her into his arms as the rest of his security parked in the driveway. She waved at Blade who was grinning like a maniac as Gavin carried her inside and slammed the front door. He kissed her long and hard.

"I love you," he said.

"I love you too."

His arms tightened to the point of pain, and his expression turned fierce.

"Don't tell me you love me unless you mean it," he warned.

Lyla brushed her nose with his. "You hurt me, but I can't stop loving you."

He dropped his head on her shoulder. "Thank you, thank you God." He raised his head and looked her straight in the eye. "I swear, baby girl, I won't let you down this time."

"I know you won't." He was different, and so was she. Death separated them twice. She wasn't going to run a third time. This time, she would fight. She would fight for Manny because it was his dying wish that she and Gavin be together. Gavin was no longer a part of the underworld, and she chose to live.

"We're going to spend the rest of the day in bed," Gavin decreed.

That sounded great to her. He carried her upstairs. When he leaned down to undo her shoes she noticed that her dress had splashes of her father's blood and her hand was swollen. She flexed it and winced.

"You want me to call a doctor?" Gavin asked, cradling her hand in his.

"No, I think I'm okay," she said and noticed that he had

blood on him as well. She must have gotten it on him when they were fucking.

"Come on," he said, helping her stand and pulling down her zipper.

The dress began to fall before she remembered her scars. She clutched the dress to her front and bit her lip as cold, hard reality seeped back. He made love to her without seeing—

"What is it?" Gavin asked.

"I... um, it isn't pretty. You may not want to see—"

Gavin gently pried her hands away from the dress and let it fall. She closed her eyes as she was left standing in only her underwear, her scars on full display. Even she could barely stand them. Gavin was used to beautiful things, and she definitely wasn't. Her chest was a representation of how she felt inside—disfigured and ugly. The silence stretched. She started to turn, but he fell to his knees, wrapped his arms around her and pressed his face against her stomach.

"Gavin—"

"I don't care about the scars," he said, and she stilled. "I'm so fucking happy that you're here with me."

He pressed his lips to the horizontal scar across her lower abdomen and traced the raised line with his tongue. Goose bumps raced over her skin as she watched him, stupefied, as he laved her scars with his tongue. *Beauty out of ashes*, she thought. He bent his head, and she saw the dried blood on his neck and it dimmed her lust. She didn't want a reminder of her father to intrude on their time together.

"Let's shower," she said.

He kissed her belly and rose. She stood under the strong spray and let him wash her hair, a habit from their past. She enjoyed the feel of his hands in her hair and returned the favor. He sat on the bench and moaned as her fingers moved over him. He really did have an amazing body. When she finished, he toweled her dry.

"I can't believe we consummated our marriage in the back of an SUV," he muttered.

Lyla flushed a little, wondering how much Blade had seen or heard. She didn't have time to ponder this because Gavin picked her up and tossed her on the bed. She bounced and watched him prowl toward her. Her breath caught as he lay beside her and traced his fingers over the scars. This was their history. There was no way to forget it. Fury, sadness, and guilt crossed over his face.

"It's okay, Gavin," she said quietly.

He splayed his hand on her stomach. "Can we still have kids?"

Her heart skipped. "What?"

"I want to have kids. We can adopt, but... can you have children?"

"I-I don't know. I didn't ask," she stammered, completely bowled over by this. A week ago, she had a hard time getting through each day, and now Gavin was asking about children. Holy crap. Talk about life moving onward. She left a funeral and might have created a new life. She wasn't on any type of birth control. She sat up and ran her hands through her tangled, damp hair.

"We'll go to a doctor," he said, rubbing his hand over her stomach. "We should know if something was damaged, or if we need to take extra precautions."

"Mmm," she said distractedly, tugging at a big knot in her hair. "Let me brush my hair."

Lyla ran to the bathroom where she grabbed her brush and attacked her hair. She couldn't stand to look at her body, so she grabbed a robe and put that on before she resumed taming the beast. Since she was in the bathroom, she brushed her teeth and was gargling mouthwash when Gavin leaned against the doorjamb. She spit out the green liquid and because she needed something else to do, began to slather lotion on her body.

"You want some?" she asked Gavin.

"No."

She was in the process of deciding whether to French braid her hair when Gavin spoke.

"You don't want to have kids?"

Her eyes flicked to his in the mirror. He was stark naked and, apparently, fine with it. Well, why shouldn't he be? He could be Brad Pitt's stunt double in Troy. Lyla played with the ends of her hair before she turned to face him. She loved the brutal, unapologetic lines of his face and the hungry look in his eyes whenever he focused on her. Gavin Pyre was a lot of man, and he was hers legally and emotionally.

"My whole focus has been to get through each day, and now you're talking about kids."

"You don't want to have kids?" he repeated.

She tapped her fingers on her thigh and imagined a little boy in Gavin's image or a little girl with her father's eyes, and her knees went weak. "I do want kids. I just didn't realize that was on the table."

"Everything's on the table," he said and pulled her against him. He ducked his head and kissed her. "I told you, I want everything that we promised each other before."

"And you want kids?"

"We don't have to have them right now, but I want to know if it's possible or not. I'm not getting any younger, and I'm out of the underworld so..."

"You want kids," she said and blew out a long breath. Holy shit. She was married, and her husband wanted kids. Most women would be jumping for joy, yet she felt as if she'd been slapped across the face. This was a huge step. They had just slept together for the first time in almost two years and the first thing on his mind was kids. For some reason, she thought of Carlo and how he got his girlfriend pregnant to marry her. She considered Gavin, wondering if he had an ulterior motive.

"You don't have to get pregnant tomorrow," he said with an easy smile she didn't trust. "I just want you to think about it."

If she didn't want to get pregnant, she needed to see a doctor for birth control. There were dozens of reasons not to get pregnant, but she didn't want to think about them now. She wrapped her arms around his neck, and he carried her back to bed. He tore off her robe, and they slid under the covers. He pulled her against him and buried his nose in her hair.

"Dad would have been so proud of you," he said.

"Manny tried to protect me that day and my dad…" She closed her eyes and fought the tears always so fucking close to the surface. "My dad couldn't care less about me. He's a selfish bastard and doesn't deserve your money or my concern. I'm done."

"I'm glad." His hand cupped her breast as if memorizing the texture and weight. "And you defended me."

She looked at him when she heard the strange note in his voice. "Of course, I did."

"You've run from me twice."

"For good reason."

"Yet you defend me in front of your family."

"You did what you've done out of loyalty, duty, and love, which makes you ten times the man my father is. He cares for no one but himself."

He stared at her for a long moment. "So you forgive me?"

"You'd kill yourself before letting harm come to Manny or me," she said solemnly. "Maybe the hit would have come even if you didn't go after Vinny's killer. We'll never know. I understand why you didn't want to let go of the underworld. I don't like it, but I get it. But you're out now, right?"

"Yes."

"Then we don't need to discuss it."

He kissed her long and deep and positioned himself between her thighs. "I love you."

He lifted her thigh and slid inside her. She moaned in delight, and he closed his eyes in ecstasy.

"I've been wanting to make love to you for over a year. I've wanted to apologize, to touch you. I didn't know if you would ever let me in again." He moved gently as his eyes opened and drilled into hers. "I won't take you for granted."

"You'd better not," she said breathlessly.

"You won't run from me again," he stated.

"No."

"Promise me, Lyla."

She wrapped a hand around his neck and pulled him down for a kiss. "You'd find me if I ran away."

He shook his head. "No, baby, I need the words."

"I won't run," she said.

"Just give me a chance. I'll make you happy."

"I'll make sure of it," Lyla said.

7

LYLA

"I DON'T HAVE to go to work today," Gavin said.

Lyla went on tiptoes and kissed him. "You have to go back sometime, and Marcus has been calling you a couple of times a day."

"He can figure it out."

"Gavin." She clasped his face between her hands. "Go. I'm going to have a girls' day with Carmen and Aunt Isabel. I'll be back before you get home."

"I'd rather you stayed here."

"I need to apologize for causing a scene at the funeral in person."

"Take your phone and don't leave Blade's sight," he ordered.

"I know. Maybe he should get a pedicure with us," she teased. She felt extremely lighthearted and carefree. Last night, Carmen accused her of being in a sex coma. Maybe she was right. Gavin spent the past three days making up for lost time. He was an insatiable beast, and she loved it. He'd worshipped her to the point of exhaustion, but the real world was calling, and they both needed to answer.

"I don't care if he gets a pedicure as long as he's armed," Gavin said.

"I'll be fine." He hesitated, and she took pity on him. She wrapped her arms around his waist. "Do you want me to call you?"

"Every hour."

"Every hour? Isn't that a bit much?"

"After losing you twice and with a killer on the loose? I don't think so."

"Aren't you going to be busy today? You don't want me interrupting—"

"That's exactly what I want you to do. It's the only way I'll be able to get anything done."

"Okay," she conceded. "Once an hour. Be expecting eight phone calls."

"Looking forward to it." He kissed her deeply and then met her eyes. "Be here when I get home."

"I will be."

He gave her another kiss before he strode toward his Aston Martin. The guards got out of his way. When he opened the driver's door, he eyed Lyla over the roof of the car. He pointed at her before he got in and peeled out of the driveway.

Blade walked up to her with a grin. "So you got him to go back to work. That's good."

She raised a brow. "He had to go back sometime."

"I thought he would go back in a month or two." Blade shrugged. "What are you up to today?"

"I'm going to have a girls' day with Carmen and her mom. I'll leave in an hour?"

"We're ready when you are."

She nodded and rushed upstairs. Gavin's staff was coming in today. He had given the staff strict orders to stay away since he brought her back. The mansion was in dire straits, thanks to their activities.

She took the time to put on makeup and do something with her hair. They were going to get the works today—hair, nails, wax. She proposed it as a way to spend time together and get their minds off Uncle Louie's death. Carmen grudgingly accepted. Lyla was armed with an unlimited credit card from Gavin.

She examined the thigh-length gray ruffle wrap dress. She gave an experimental twirl in the mirror and realized she was smiling. It was amazing the difference a week could make. A week ago, she was contemplating whether her life was worth living. Now, she was married and looking forward to her future. Gavin made an appointment with a gynecologist who had been horrified when she took in Lyla's scarred abdomen. The doctor requested Lyla's hospital records and verified that no vital organs had been damaged. She should be able to get pregnant, but they would monitor her closely to make sure everything went okay. Despite this reassurance, Lyla requested oral contraception. Gavin didn't comment, but his expressionless face said it all. She didn't want to rush into anything and was going to pick up the prescription tomorrow.

Lyla was halfway down the stairs when her phone rang. She fetched it out of her purse and shook her head when she saw the name on the screen.

"Hello," she said.

"It's been an hour," Gavin said.

"I haven't even left the house yet."

"We agreed, every hour."

"I'm surprised you didn't insist we video chat," she said as she made her way to the foyer.

A pause and then, "That would be even better."

"Gavin, I'm walking out the door. I'll call you in an hour."

"Tell me," he said.

She knew what he wanted. He demanded she say it several times a day. "I love you."

"I love you too, baby girl."

Lyla walked down the steps and climbed into the back of the SUV. She had to resist the urge to look in the trunk to see if there was any sign of their consummation. She would never be able to ride in this SUV without remembering their hot sex session. She texted Carmen that she was on her way and got an unpleasant reply—her mother was at Aunt Isabel's house. She ignored the knots in her stomach. She hadn't changed her mind about taking away her parents' allowance. It wasn't Gavin's duty to support them. Her father had embezzled, and if he couldn't get a job as an accountant, he had to find another career. How many times had he dragged Lyla and her mother down with him? He would never change. Her connection to the Pyres made her father feel entitled to more money as if Gavin should pay him a dowry or something.

Blade helped her out when they parked in Aunt Isabel's driveway. She walked up to the front door with three guards. The door was answered by Carmen who looked annoyed. She reached out and dragged Lyla into a tight hug.

"You're really okay?" Carmen asked.

"Yes. Are you ready to go?"

Carmen gave her a put upon look. "Your mother's been here since six, crying and carrying on."

Lyla straightened her shoulders. "Where is she?"

Carmen led her into the kitchen while the guards stayed in the living room. Her mother sat at a small dining table. She looked awful with puffy eyes, unbrushed hair, and a pile of used tissues in front of her. When she spotted Lyla, she rushed over.

"Lyla, Daddy told me you took away our money. How are we going to live?" Mom wailed.

"He needs to find a job."

"But you know it's going to be hard for him after the misunderstanding at Pyre Casinos."

Lyla cocked her head to the side. "Misunderstanding? It wasn't a misunderstanding, Mom, he *stole* half a million."

"Daddy said—"

"He's a liar and a gambling addict," Lyla said succinctly, shocking her mother into silence. "I asked Gavin to let you two live off a generous allowance. He didn't have to do that. He never asked Dad to repay anything he stole. At the funeral, Dad asked for more money so he could gamble."

"He needs something to do," Mom said imploringly.

"Gambling isn't a hobby. It's an addiction. If he needs money to gamble, why hasn't he tried to get a job for side income?"

"He's still recovering from when they beat him up," Mom said a bit indignantly.

Lyla shook her head. "He insulted me and the Pyres. He has no respect for anyone, so why should I have respect for him? You and Dad need to figure it out."

Mom's mouth dropped open. Lyla's calm delivery had clearly stunned her.

"But what if he can't get another job?"

"That's his problem. If you need a place to stay, you can always come to me, but Dad isn't welcome."

"He's your father, Lyla."

"Calling me a slut and a whore doesn't make me feel charitable toward him, especially when I gave up everything to save his ass when he embezzled."

"He can be callous sometimes, but—"

"No, Mom, I'm done." Lyla looked at Aunt Isabel who was clearly fascinated by the conversation. "Hi, Aunty, you ready?"

"You can't just do this to us!" Mom burst out. "You have a responsibility to take care of us."

"When you can't take care of yourselves, I will, out of duty," Lyla said dispassionately. "But right now, if he can run his mouth as easily as he does, he can make a living."

"You've changed," Mom said accusingly.

"Yes, I have."

"I don't know what you've become, but you aren't the daughter I raised."

Lyla stared at her. "You haven't asked where I've been for the past year and a half."

"What?"

"You haven't asked how I am, where I've been, if I'm happy. Parents who cared would ask." Lyla waited for her mother to say something, but she'd been struck dumb. "Let's go, Aunt Isabel."

Lyla walked out of the house and was joined in the back of the SUV by Aunt Isabel and Carmen. Aunt Isabel took her hand and squeezed.

"Your parents care in their own way," she said.

Lyla gave her a weak smile. "That's not important. How are you?"

"Getting on. I'm glad Carmen's here. I haven't been good company."

"It'll take time," Lyla said and then, "I'm sorry for what happened between me and my dad. I shouldn't have—"

"I heard what he said. If you hadn't done something, Gavin would have, and he had every right to," Aunt Isabel said. "If Louie heard your father, he would have whooped his ass too."

"I don't know what came over me."

"Years of pent-up frustration, probably. Pat never treated you right, and you've always been so sweet."

Carmen snickered. "That was awesome. He's been begging for it for years. Dad would have been proud."

They chatted until they reached the salon. Carmen air kissed the cheek of the owner, and Lyla did the same. It seemed like a lifetime since they had been here last. The hairdressers were clucking over the state of their hair when Lyla's phone rang again. She picked up as she leaned into a large lit up mirror.

"Hi," she said.

"You're frying my nerves here," Gavin growled.

"Sorry. We just got to the salon." She fluffed her hair. "You think I'll look cute with pink hair?"

"Come again?"

"Pink hair? Short hair?"

"Don't dye your hair. It's gorgeous, and I like it the way it is. Blade said your mom was at the house. Trouble?"

"No. I took care of it."

"You okay?"

"Yes."

"Call me in an hour. I love you."

"I love you too."

They hung up, and she set the alarm on her phone. A hairdresser with bulging breasts barely contained by her apron dragged her fingers through Lyla's hair.

"What can I do for you, darling?"

"I'm going to be boring. Just trim and condition, please," Lyla said.

"You sure? I can do great things with your hair."

"My... husband likes it as is," Lyla said, stumbling over the h word.

"I can see why," the hairdresser said and held her hair up to the light. "Women would kill for this shade."

Aunt Isabel dyed her silver hair an auburn shade and paired the color with a short cut that wouldn't take much time to style. Lyla was speechless when Carmen dyed her blonde hair black. The stark color against her pale skin and blue eyes was a startling contrast that changed her whole demeanor. During her blow dry, Blade came over with the phone. Lyla apologized to Gavin and tried to convince him that she set the alarm but didn't hear it. He wasn't pleased. When they went to get their mani and pedis, Carmen chose pointed maroon nails that went with her biker chick vibe. Lyla went with modest rose-colored nails while Aunt Isabel got a French tip.

"How are you?" Lyla asked Carmen.

"I'm fine," she said loftily.

"Carmen."

"What?"

Lyla took in Carmen's drastic new look and saw beneath the nonchalant attitude to the pain beneath. "What are your plans?"

"Can't make any without money," Carmen said archly.

"You're right. I'll talk to Gavin about it."

"Did you know Mr. Important wants to pay for Dad's funeral?" Carmen asked with a sneer.

She tried to hold onto her temper. She left the house this morning with a great attitude, but it was deteriorating rapidly. She wished she asked Gavin to stay home and hibernate for another day in their love nest.

"He wants to help," Lyla said.

"If he gave me my money, I could pay for it myself."

"I know. Just let Gavin pay for it, and I swear, I'll talk to him about your money tonight."

"So you forgave him for everything?"

"Everything?" Lyla asked, and the manicurist tugged on her fingers, which were trying to ball into a fist.

Carmen's eyes dipped down to Lyla's concealed chest. "You left him for a reason."

"I did," Lyla said, striving for calm. "He hurt me; I hurt him. We've both made mistakes, but I've always loved him."

"Just because you love each other doesn't mean you're meant to be together. You must have some reservations. I mean, he hasn't changed much. He forced you to marry him."

"Yes," she said and blew out a breath. "He won't allow any distance between us."

"His love is toxic."

"Carmen," Lyla snapped and glared at her cousin. "I love you. Please, just, don't. I know what I'm doing." She didn't know how to explain the need in Gavin's eyes, the way he held her almost desperately close. She owed Carmen so much, yet she couldn't let her cousin derail her relationship with Gavin.

They finished their manicures in silence while Aunt Isabel's manicurist told raunchy jokes. Lyla felt like a million dollars by the time they left the salon. She called Gavin on their way to a restaurant.

"Hey, you," she said.

"Hey. What color is your hair?"

"Still blonde."

"Good. Length?"

"Long enough."

"Lyla?"

"Yes?" she teased.

"I miss you."

"I miss you too. Can you call in tomorrow?"

"Yes."

He didn't hesitate. She'd had a hell of a day so far, and she didn't want to leave her bed tomorrow.

"Is Marcus gonna hate me?" she asked.

"Doesn't matter."

"It does, Gavin. I know you need to work. No, you should go in tomorrow. I'm just going to sleep all day."

"And I can keep you company."

Even while that appealed to her, she said, "How about you go in for a half day so I don't feel so selfish?"

"Deal. Where are you now?"

"We're going to have a late lunch."

"Okay. Love you."

"Love you too."

They had a pleasant lunch. Aunt Isabel had color in her cheeks, and although she had an unexpected breakdown during the meal, she was in good spirits. Lyla couldn't take her eyes off Carmen who was drawing just as much attention with black hair as she had as a blonde. She looked edgy and a tad dangerous. Was she doing it on purpose? Lyla didn't know what to make of her transformation. Carmen sneered when Lyla excused herself to call Gavin again. By the time they arrived back at Aunt Isabel's house, Lyla was satisfied but exhausted. She hugged Aunt Isabel and told her if she needed anything, to call her. Lyla wasn't surprised when Carmen saw her to the door.

"I can see you're happy," Carmen said and shrugged. "I'm just... scared for you."

"I know."

Carmen swallowed hard. "I miss Vinny and my dad."

Lyla hugged her. "I know. I miss them too."

"I can't lose you too."

"You won't."

"You can't guarantee that."

"Gavin won't let anyone touch me. You know that, right?"

Carmen sighed. "I went from this house to life with Vinny, and now I'm back to square one. What am I supposed to do with my life?"

"You can do whatever you want, but I hope you stay in Vegas with me."

"After being on the road, it's nice to be in one place and have space," Carmen said as she drew back and wiped her wet cheeks.

"Definitely." Lyla braced her hands on her cousin's shoulders. "I'm going to talk to Gavin about your money. I want to be involved in whatever you do next. If you guys need anything, I'm here, okay?"

Carmen nodded. "I'm glad you finally stood up to your parents. Manny's death changed you for the better."

Why did it always take a tragedy to invoke change?

"I don't know what goes on with you and Gavin, and I don't want to. I know he loves you. He always has and, apparently, always will." Carmen's eyes filled with tears. "The way he watched you at the funeral... it's the way my dad looked at my mom, the way Vinny looked at me, but Gavin... He's a completely different ball game. He doesn't have the sweetness that Vinny did. Gavin can be ruthless and cruel, and you've never been a match for him." Carmen leaned back and considered her. "Maybe now you are."

"I hope so." Lyla hesitated before she asked, "After all that's happened, do you think we can have normal lives?"

"You, maybe. If Gavin keeps his nose clean and he keeps worshipping the ground you walk on." Carmen fluffed her black tresses. "Me? I don't know."

"Why not?"

Carmen's lower lip trembled before she controlled it. "I loved Vinny with everything in me. Who's lucky enough to love like that twice in a lifetime? It might kill me."

For the first time in a long time, Lyla thought of Jonathan, the gentle IT consultant who had coaxed her into a relationship. Her affection for him couldn't be compared to what she shared with Gavin. It was like trying to compare a kitten to a tiger. No, she couldn't imagine having what she had with Gavin with another man.

"I'm here for you," Lyla said.

Carmen nodded and hugged her again. "I love you."

"I don't know what I would have done without you. I owe you everything."

"It was my pleasure," Carmen said with a watery smile and bowed.

"You're crazy, you know that?" Lyla laughed as Carmen sashayed away.

Exhausted by the time they reached home, Lyla went upstairs and drew a bath. She moaned as she climbed into the tub and closed her eyes. She understood Carmen's worry. Most would think she was a glutton for punishment, but no one saw what she did in Gavin. He was rough around the edges—animalistic, merciless, and savage. But there was also gentleness in him and a craving for touch and love—*her* touch, *her* love. Aunt Isabel and Carmen couldn't hide the crippling pain of losing their men. Lyla didn't have to ask to know the answer. Neither woman regretted their time with their husbands. They would take the pain and live with it for the rest of their lives, knowing it was a small price to pay for the memories.

"Baby?"

She opened tear-drenched eyes and blinked up at

Gavin. A sob escaped. He crouched down and kissed her. She gripped his wrists and then twisted her hand in his shirt, dragging him down so she could feel him against her. Gavin lost his clothes, climbed in the tub, and hovered over her.

"Tell me you won't leave me," she said.

Gavin pulled back. "What?"

"Vinny, Uncle Louie, and Manny. They didn't plan on dying. I can't lose you too. You can't die."

"I'm not going to die."

"They might come for you and—"

"Lyla, I'm not going anywhere."

"You promise?"

"I promise."

"Make me believe."

His mouth latched on hers. He sat and pulled her astride him.

"I need," Lyla said, reaching down to position him.

He spread his hands on either side of the bathtub, eyes alight with excitement. "Take me."

She moved on his cock, absorbing the feel of him inside her. He was hers to touch and explore. She didn't know how to explain the need for comfort after being with Carmen and Aunt Isabel. Their grief was etched on them for all time. She needed the connection with Gavin, the reassurance she wasn't alone. Her man was here, and she would fight to keep him.

"I love you," Lyla said as she moved on him. "I always have."

Gavin's hungry, starved eyes watched her every move.

"I can run, but my heart and mind always knew you would come for me."

"Always," he said through gritted teeth, muscles flexing.

"I don't want a marriage like everyone else. I want a marriage that suits us."

He gave a jerky nod. Lyla rode him harder, splashing water heedlessly over the sides. His eyes went blind a moment before he gripped her hips and shoved himself all the way inside her. Lyla screamed and climaxed a moment before he did. Gavin rested his face in the hollow of her neck as she panted. His hands moved lazily over her.

"You have to know something about me," he said.

Lyla tried to move back to see his face, but she was too exhausted. "What?"

"I won't give you up."

She chuckled. "You do whatever you have to keep that promise."

"I will." His hands moved over her. "Did you have a good day?"

"Yes and no. You?"

"Same."

"You hungry?"

"Yeah."

"Give me a minute and I'll remember how to walk."

Gavin rose and set her on the vanity bench to towel her dry. They dressed in robes and went downstairs where a delicious roast was waiting for them. They made their plates and sat at the table. She told Gavin about her mother and her day with Carmen and Aunt Isabel. He reciprocated with Marcus's ideas for Pyre Casinos and how he was becoming an excellent asset and partner. Lyla was pleased. Maybe they could have a normal life after murder and mayhem.

They retired to the couch where Gavin propped her feet on his lap and massaged them gently. She tipped her head back and moaned. When she opened her eyes, she saw that Gavin was focused on her gaping robe. She ignored the fire in her belly and said, "You need to give Carmen's money back to her."

His hands paused.

"You have no right to control her money. Vinny wouldn't like it either. She needs the freedom to do what she wants, especially after losing her dad and husband."

Gavin had a strange look on his face. Lyla wriggled her toes impatiently.

"What are her plans?" he asked.

"I don't know, and it's none of our business."

"I want to know what her plan is before I give her the money."

"Why?" Lyla asked and then her intuition pinged. "You don't want to give her the money because you think we'll run again?"

A muscle clenched in his cheek. "I told you, I'm not taking chances with you."

"What the hell was that in the tub? I just committed myself to you ten times over! You can't punish Carmen for the choices I make. *I* asked her to get me out, and she did. She's my cousin and saw me get diced up by a psycho. Of course, she's gonna get me out. She loves me."

"I'm not going to give her money so she can cause trouble."

"Believe it or not, Carmen respects us. Besides that, how many times have I promised to stay?" She spread her arms wide. "I'm here, Gavin."

"Because I forced you."

His words stung. She withdrew her feet from his lap and sat up. "So you don't trust me."

"I don't want her to tempt you."

"I promised you I wouldn't run."

Gavin's eyes were hot with conflicting emotions.

"I'm not playing you. I'm here, and I'm not going anywhere."

"Give me a guarantee," he said.

"I have nothing to offer but my word! You either trust me or you don't. I have to trust you won't cheat on me or decide to go back to the underworld."

"Low blow, Lyla."

"I'm not interested in sugarcoating anything, Gavin. It's too late for that. We have to trust each other."

She walked toward the staircase but didn't get far. On the first stair, he hauled her backward.

"*Don't* walk away from me," he growled in her ear.

"Don't be such a jackass!" she countered as he strode back to the couch and tossed her on it. She bounced on the plush cushions and grunted when Gavin came down on top of her. "You can't control everyone."

"I can try."

Lyla huffed. "You can't do that to Carmen. It's not fair."

His hands sank into her hair and gripped. "I just got you back. I don't want Carmen distracting you or making you wonder if you're better off with her again."

"You have to trust me. Do you?"

His expression was tormented. "I want to."

"But you don't."

His hand cupped her nape and squeezed. "I want all of you."

"You have me."

He parted her robe, uncovering her abdomen. His hand splayed over her scarred stomach.

"Are you sure of me?" he asked.

She was, right? As the silence stretched, his fingers twitched.

"If you trust me, why'd you ask for birth control?"

She tried to shove him off her, but he didn't budge. "That's my choice, Gavin!"

"Why do you want to prevent pregnancy?"

"Because we shouldn't rush into having kids. We have a lot of issues to work through first."

"Like?"

"Like what kind of life we're going to have in a month! You just went back to work today. I had to call you every hour. That's not normal, Gavin."

"You know why I'm doing it."

"I get it, but you can't tell a kid to do that. Or maybe you want to homeschool it because you can't stand to have the kid be away from you? You can't make a kid a prisoner, Gavin."

His eyes narrowed. "You feel like a prisoner?"

"At first, yes, but I want to be your captive so..."

"So what are we talking about?"

"We're talking about your need for control. I don't know if you're going to ease up in a few weeks or never."

"Dad's killer is still on the loose."

"Yet I can get a full night's sleep without worrying about that, and I'm the one who looked into his eyes." She shuddered. "We can't stop living because of him. We need to *live*. That's what Manny would have wanted for us."

"And living means trying for a baby," he said implacably.

Her stomach iced. "I don't want to bring anyone into our situation unless it's stable."

"Meaning I'm not?"

"Neither of us are. I could drop into depression and so could you. We don't know how this marriage is going to work or how the underworld is going to handle you being out of the game. There are so many variables."

"As you said, we can't live our lives based on other

people's agenda. We need to do what we want regardless of those factors. In my mind, our life is gonna be like this: I wake up with you, make love to you, and go to work. You do whatever you want during the day. I come home; I want you here. We eat, shower, and fuck. I fall asleep with you wrapped around me. That's what I plan for us. What about you?"

She didn't know what to say. He stroked her stomach, and when his eyes met hers, she caught her breath at the hunger there.

"When I was in jail, I had a dream that we had a daughter who looked exactly like you. I walked in the front door, and this little girl ran to me. I picked her up. She was so small and full of life. She covered my faces with kisses and told me I needed to help her make cookies. Her name was Nora."

"Your mother's name?" Her heart wrenched at the image he painted in her mind.

"Yes. She was so real. I know exactly what she was wearing, the smell of her hair, the weight of her against my chest. Even now, I have feelings for her, and she doesn't exist."

Her eyes filled with tears. This man knew how to rip her heart out. She heard the yearning in his voice and ached to give him what he wanted. "You're killing me here."

"I love you," he said fiercely. "No one will ever love you as I do."

He was telling the truth. It wasn't possible for any man to love her more than Gavin Pyre did.

"Our kids will be my redemption, my way to make up for all the shit I've done. In my mind, we need kids to move forward, or we're going to keep sliding backward. Nora was..." He shook his head, and she saw his eyes glint with tears. "Beautiful. Pure. I need that in my life."

"No pressure on me," she said faintly.

"You don't need to worry about it. It'll happen," he said with complete confidence.

"How do you know?"

"The same way I knew you were meant for me the moment I met you, the way I know God spared you because I couldn't live without you. This is why we're here... to create good out of the hell we've been through."

Lyla brushed away a tear and then thumped him on the shoulder. "How do you do this to me?"

"Do what?"

"Wreck me, convince me to believe in the impossible."

"It's a gift." He searched her face. "You understand why I want to try?"

"Yes."

"Are we going to?"

She tossed a hand over her face, seeing the image he created so vividly in her mind. A little girl who pressed kisses over Gavin's face, demanding he make cookies with her. Everything in her yearned to give that to him and herself. A child... "Yes."

Gavin kissed her hard. "Thank you."

"Are you going to give Carmen her money?"

"Yes," he said as he spread her robe wide and positioned himself between her legs. He lifted her thighs on his shoulders and slid his tongue over her. "I missed your taste."

Lyla locked her ankles around his back and clutched the couch cushions.

"Are you on the pill?" he asked, voice muffled as he talked against her.

"No."

"Good."

He sat up and positioned himself between her legs. The

slide of his cock made her insides quiver and burn as she stretched. She shivered beneath him as he slid in all the way. He shuddered as if he couldn't handle the sensation and pumped his hips.

"If we have a girl, can we name her after my mom?"

As if she would deny him after hearing his dream. "Of course," she panted.

He kissed her, smearing her taste on her lips. She whimpered as he ground into her.

"Thank you," he whispered.

"You do know we may not have a girl or even get pregnant?"

"We will have kids," he said firmly. "And we will have a girl."

Knowing she wasn't protected and that he was trying to get her pregnant made her hot. *Really* hot. "Fuck me, Gavin."

He gave her a feral smile. "Don't mind if I do."

He didn't hold back. He fucked her as if his life depended on it, as if this was the last time he would have sex in his life. He fucked her so hard that she screamed and clawed at his chest. She begged him to stop and then begged for more. Gavin didn't let up until she convulsed around him. He came seconds later, planting himself as deep as possible and filling her with him.

8

GAVIN

Lyla was getting restless. She didn't say so, but Gavin noticed and it made him uneasy. It had been four months since he brought her back from Montana. He gave Carmen access to her money, and to his relief, she made no drastic moves and continued to live with her mother. Lyla spent three days a week with Carmen and Aunt Isabel, either hanging out at their house or going out to do girl things. Carmen joined Lyla at the gun range. Blade reported that their skills were progressing quickly.

He was able to pull back on his need to have Lyla call him every hour when she was out of the house, but he couldn't resist checking the house cameras when she was home. If she knew how much he watched her, she would freak, but he couldn't help it. He needed constant access to her to get anything done. He was back to working fifty hours a week, and it felt good. At times, he reached for the phone to call Vinny before he remembered he wasn't there.

The rumors surrounding the money laundering and his father's murder made their casino a notorious hotspot, and they were raking in stupid cash. Marcus made improvements in the clubs and subtle updates to the casino that made all the difference in the world. For the first time in his life, he was able to think about something else besides business, and that something was his wife.

He knew a psychologist would have a field day with him. His love was an obsession, but that was nothing new. Lyla had captivated him from the start. He resented her hold on him until she left, making him realize how worthless his life was without her. He held nothing back now. He claimed her every chance he had to reinforce their bond, to ensure she knew he loved her. The need to shower her with gifts was wasted on her since she wanted nothing. The first three months were rocky with both of them waking from nightmares in a cold sweat. Lyla had bouts of depression that kept her in bed for days at a time. He didn't mind staying home to care for her. Marcus didn't question his absences from work. Every day that he loved her out of the darkness, she bloomed, and when she smiled at him with her eyes shining, he could barely breathe. He felt drunk on her, addicted to her smiles and laughter and love. He steeped himself in her, and it kept his demons at bay.

The cops were monitoring him, but for the first time in his life, he was clean as a whistle. He put out lures to see if the underworld would reveal the new crime lord's identity, but nothing came back. Not a whisper, which made him sick with worry. There were always rats in the underworld, greedy fuckers who would sell their own children for a profit. What made this new crime lord untouchable, and why was everyone more afraid of this fucker than of him? The unanswered questions tortured him, making him all the more protective of Lyla who, thankfully, didn't buck against him yet. He didn't sleep as much as he should. He spent most nights holding Lyla against him and plotting the murder of the faceless man who dared challenge him.

Gavin clicked on his computer screen and accessed the security cameras around the house. Although half of her week was taken up, Lyla spent most days cleaning (even though they had a maid), swimming, or pacing. She spent a lot of time in his office where his father's ashes were. He didn't intrude on their time together.

He asked if she wanted to go on a trip, but she declined. He was running out of things to distract her. Lyla didn't complain, but he sensed her growing agitation. She was recovering physically and mentally from the trauma, and with that came more energy, which she didn't have an outlet for. He was trying his damnedest to get her pregnant not only to make his dream of having a daughter a reality, but also to bind her more tightly to him. Lyla was softhearted, caring, and loving. A child would flourish under her care. He knew it and couldn't wait to have her pregnant with his child. It would be a girl. God wouldn't give him such a dream unless he would make it come true.

Gavin scowled as he clicked through the cameras and didn't see his wife. She hadn't told him she was going out today. Maybe Carmen called her? He called her cell. No answer. He called Blade who also didn't answer. A fine layer of sweat covered his body as panic sank in. He got to his feet and was about to call another member of his wife's personal security when his secretary buzzed him. He was about to tell her to fuck off, but before he could do so, the door opened.

Lyla walked in, dressed in a skirt that showed off her legs, a deep orange blouse, and a trench coat. He shot up from his chair.

"Why the fuck didn't you answer my call?" Didn't she

know how much she meant to him? Didn't she know he would fucking lose it if she disappeared?

She closed the door and walked toward him. "Gavin, I was two minutes away from your office. I came to surprise you. Do you want to eat lunch?"

"You *don't* fucking ignore my calls, got it?"

Lyla crossed her arms and frowned at him. "What's wrong with you?"

"You and Blade didn't answer! What am I supposed to think? You never told me you were going anywhere."

"That's what a surprise is," she said slowly.

"I don't fucking like surprises."

"Apparently."

He closed the distance between them, buried his shaking hands in her hair and kissed her. She had no idea what he was capable of, no idea the control he had to exert to keep himself from sliding into destruct mode. The violence he once channeled into the underworld dealings, he released in the boxing ring with UFC fighters. When he could, he lost the business suit and trained. The physical exertion made his rage manageable, but it kept coming back. Lyla was the only person on the planet that made him feel normal. The moment he was away from her, he was restless, savage, and less human.

Lyla kissed him back, and it fired his blood. He placed her on the desk and thrust two fingers into her. She gripped his shirt and moaned into his mouth. He growled in satisfaction when he found her soaked for him.

"Did you come for this?" he asked, pulling back so he could see her face.

"I was going to let you have me after lunch," she said and spread her thighs wide, showing him her black lace underwear.

"I'll have you then, too," he decided on the spot as he unzipped his pants and slid inside her. Lyla belonged to him. Every inch, every breath. He was her master and slave. He slid inside her and shivered as she closed around him. Every morning, every night, he took her. He couldn't get enough. No other woman could do this to him. The others had been cheap imitations of sex, but this—this was heaven on earth. Their souls spoke to one another in the aftermath, and every time he claimed her, he renewed their vows.

"I've been missing you," she said, framing his face with her small hands.

"Good," he grunted as he sank in to the hilt. "I want you to miss me every second I'm not with you."

"Did you miss me?"

He didn't know how to tell her what she meant to him without scaring the shit out of her. "Always."

She moved his shirt aside to suck on his neck. "I like distracting you at work and getting you all hot and bothered."

"Anytime," he said and looked down at the delectable angel on his desk being impaled by his rock-hard cock. "This should be a part of my schedule."

"You'll get tired of it."

Gavin nipped her bottom lip. "I assure you, I will never get tired of you. Ever."

Lyla smiled, and he couldn't help himself. He began to thrust hard, deep, and fast. After the fucking scare she gave him, he couldn't go slow. He gorged on her, and she writhed against him.

"Fuck me, Gavin. Take me," she panted.

"Fucking tell me who you belong to," he ground out.

"You."

He gripped her hair and tilted her head back so he could bite the base of her neck. "I need to plant a baby in you."

"Do it."

He bit her neck as he pumped into her. God, he wanted nothing more than to see her pregnant, her body becoming full and lush with the continuation of life. He thought it would calm him somewhat, knowing his daughter was on the way, but it hadn't happened yet. On the other hand, he had no problem seeing to it that Lyla was properly filled with cum every chance he got.

He pinched her clit, and she convulsed around him. He jerked her to the edge of the desk as he came, grinding into her and pouring all he had inside her. He tipped her head back and loved the glazed, sated look on her face.

"Tell me you love me," he demanded.

"I love you."

He kissed her because he couldn't get enough. Lyla didn't stop him even though her lips were swollen and bruised by the time he felt sane.

"Have I ruined you?" he asked, pulling away so he could scan her clothes.

"Completely," she said with a wicked grin, and he smiled back. "But I seem to be presentable."

She pushed him away and went to the bathroom to clean up while he watched.

"You told Blade not to answer his phone," he guessed as his mind flashed back to his earlier panic.

"Yes." Lyla turned and wagged her finger at him. "Don't punish him for that."

"He doesn't take orders from you."

When she stiffened, he inwardly cursed. Her silver blue eyes flashed in anger, replacing her satisfied look.

"Excuse me?" she asked in a dangerous voice.

"Your safety is—"

"Not in question," she said crisply. "We were a few yards from your office or else I would have allowed him to pick up your call."

"I don't care how close you are. He isn't allowed to ignore my call."

"Gavin, nothing happened."

"I need to know where you are at all times. I need your security guard to pick up his fucking phone."

"Blade managed to call you even though he'd been shot five times," Lyla snapped. "You think he wouldn't call you if my life was in danger?"

If he wanted Lyla to visit him again, he had to put this shit to the side. Nothing happened and she wanted to surprise him. He shouldn't bitch. For now.

"Come here," he said, holding his hand out to her.

"No."

He shook his head and went to her. She knocked his hand away, showing him that her sparring sessions with Blade were working. She was becoming quite the little fighter, and it aroused him. He never believed that the young innocent he claimed at eighteen would morph into the woman she was today.

He put his hand around her nape and hauled her close. She glared mutinously up at him.

"Thank you for the surprise. I enjoyed it," he said.

Lyla snorted.

"I won't punish Blade, but I don't want you countering my instructions, especially when I nearly had a heart attack when neither of you answered."

"Fine. I'll let him tell you a white lie next time."

He didn't like that either, but he didn't want to argue about it now. "Let's eat."

She mumbled something under her breath and then caught sight of his computer screen, which had live feeds of the bedroom, living room, and pool.

"You watch me?" she asked.

He spread his hands and raked his mind for an acceptable answer. "I check on you every now and then."

"And you didn't think to mention it?"

"No."

Lyla shook her head. "You are unbelievable."

"Lyla—"

"No."

She walked out of the office. He saw Blade and a team of six waiting for them. Blade met his glare head-on. They would have words later, but he wouldn't punish him since the result had been pleasurable, and it was his fault for leaving the live security feed on his computer. He wanted to haul her back into the office, but she was fuming and might make a scene if he did. God, this woman was going to kill him.

Marcus approached, eyes focused on Lyla. Gavin wanted to throw his hands up in frustration. He thought he had control over things and now his day was being royally fucked.

"I heard a rumor you were here," Marcus said as he took Lyla's hand. "I'm glad we finally get to meet."

"And you are?" Lyla asked.

"This is Marcus, my COO," Gavin said grudgingly.

Lyla and Marcus were sizing each other up, and it struck him that they were around the same age, unlike him who was almost ten years older. Lyla's fair beauty complemented Marcus's All-American good looks. His hands balled into fists as the silence stretched.

"Gavin told me a lot about you," Lyla said finally. "I hear you're doing great things for the company."

"Yes, and I'm glad you're doing well enough for Mr. Pyre to come back to work," Marcus said.

Lyla nodded and glanced at Gavin before she said, "You should join us for lunch."

Before Gavin could decline for him, Marcus accepted. "My pleasure."

Gavin's chest locked as Marcus offered his arm. She took it without hesitation, leaving Gavin behind as they walked away. Blade placed a hand on his heaving chest.

"Cool it, Gavin," he cautioned.

Gavin shrugged him off and went after his COO and wife. It wasn't rational that he was insanely jealous of her being able to converse with another man. He'd claimed her before anyone had a chance and had always been aware of that fact. Seeing her with Marcus made him lightheaded with fury. Just when he was about to pound his fist into his partner's face, he registered what Lyla was saying.

Lyla had worked as his father's personal assistant for a little over a year. He'd assumed she did filing, scheduling, and phone calls. He was struck speechless by the managerial tasks his father issued to her and the depth of her involvement in company projects that had since become a reality. Her knowledge of the company shocked him. Marcus began to pick her brain while Gavin walked mutely by her side. Lyla's face lit up as he bounced ideas off her. Gavin was torn between pride at her insight and irritation that he hadn't thought to ask for her opinion. Why didn't he talk to her more about work? It was obvious Lyla was intelligent and knowledgeable, thanks to his father.

Marcus led Lyla into one of the five restaurants in the casino and acknowledged the hostess before he chose a booth in the quietest corner possible during the lunch rush. Gavin was hard pressed not to grab Marcus by the collar and fling him when he scooted into the booth after his wife. To compound his sins, Marcus turned toward Lyla, elbow on the table as she spoke. Blade nudged Gavin in the side, a warning to keep his head before taking a seat at another table.

The server interrupted Lyla and Marcus's intense conversation. Gavin ordered whiskey to drown out the unreasonable jealousy fizzing in his veins. Lyla gave him an odd look before Marcus claimed her attention again. Marcus was a relentless businessman—keen, ruthless, and sharp. Gavin respected the hell out of him, but at the moment, he wanted to kill him.

"What are you doing this Friday?" Marcus asked.

Gavin's temper went black. "Are you asking my wife out?"

"Well, yes," Marcus said with a shrug. "She should be at the opening of our new nightclub, Incognito."

"My wife doesn't go out," Gavin said through gritted teeth.

"Why...? Oh." Marcus's expression sobered. "Forgive me. I understand. You mustn't be comfortable going out after—"

"Actually, I would love to go," Lyla said, shocking the hell out of Gavin. "What time should I be there? Are you going to pick me up?"

"Fuck that." Gavin reached across the table to grab Marcus when a woman tapped him on the shoulder.

"Scoot in, will you? I need to talk to you both about the press release for Incognito," Janice said.

Gavin scooted to the middle of the booth so he could yank Lyla away from Marcus. He clamped a hand on her thigh and glared at Marcus who gave him a puzzled look as if he couldn't figure out why he was so steamed.

"Have we met?" Janice asked Lyla.

"This is my wife," Gavin said.

Janice's mouth sagged. She looked Lyla over and beamed. "Are you coming to the opening of Incognito? Your face will photograph great and next to Gavin, you'll look stunning! This will be great publicity."

"That's exactly what I was thinking," Marcus said. "She used to be Manny Pyre's personal assistant, you know."

"No, I didn't," Janice said and stopped the server to order herself a meal. "That's fascinating."

His staff was looking at Lyla as if she were Mother Teresa. Janice had a hell of a time trying to polish his tarnished image, not that he cared. Marcus did, and it was obvious they wanted to use Lyla to make him do appearances and shit.

"I found you. Yay!" Alice, the Community Outreach Coordinator, sat beside Janice. "Are you discussing what's going to happen on Friday? I know we're scheduled for a meeting tomorrow, but if we're all here... Oh, hi. Sorry, have we met?"

"This is Lyla, Gavin's wife," Janice explained. "She used to work with Manny Pyre."

"Is that right? Which projects were you involved in?" Alice asked.

Gavin wanted to bang his head on the table. Everyone ignored him and focused on his wife. He should have expected this. With the way Lyla stayed out of the public eye and the rumors surrounding the day his father was killed, it was only natural for them to be curious about her. Add Lyla's beauty, age, and obvious intelligence and everyone was hooked on her. Gavin listened as Lyla outlined the projects she'd been involved in and noticed Janice and Alice exchange looks.

Lunch was served. Gavin firmly turned the conversation back to Janice's plans for Incognito's opening. He had planned to stop by to make sure all was well, but now it looked like he'd be there all night. Lyla listened attentively and even clarified some key points that made Janice blink in surprise.

"Are you looking for a job?" Marcus asked bluntly.

Lyla flushed. "Actually—"

"No," Gavin snapped.

Lyla turned to him. "Excuse me?"

"You're not getting a job."

Lyla turned back to their fascinated audience. "I'll get back to you on that."

He wanted to strangle Marcus who slapped his hand on the table and roared with laughter. He wanted to haul Lyla out of the restaurant and cart her back to his office where he would show her who was the boss. Instead, he was forced to sit there and act as if his blood wasn't boiling. Lyla seemed completely at ease, eating and chatting with his staff as if they were old friends.

"I'd like to help you with outreach," Lyla said to Alice, who looked excited until she glanced at his face.

By the time lunch was over, he could barely contain himself. Marcus kissed Lyla's hand and took off at a trot, talking to his secretary on his phone as he went. Janice and Alice both shook Lyla's hand and said they would see her on Friday before they took off.

"I'm taking her home," Gavin said to Blade.

Lyla looked up as he clamped a hand on her waist. "What? Why?"

Gavin didn't say a thing as he led her through the casino.

They took the elevator down to the parking garage. She gave him a strange look before she got into the Aston Martin. He revved the engine and liked the sound of the car's squealing tires as he drove into traffic.

"Is there a reason you're driving me home?" Lyla asked.

"We need to talk," he said, flexing his hands on the wheel.

"About what?"

"Do you find Marcus attractive?"

She turned in her seat toward him. "Are you fucking serious?"

"You let him touch you, and you were hanging on every word he said." Yeah, he sounded like a possessive bastard, but he couldn't help it. He couldn't stand seeing another man touch her or enjoy her company. It made him feel homicidal, thinking that she might have chemistry with another man. He wouldn't allow it.

"I still have your cum inside me," she said.

The unexpected comment made him glance at her. She looked furious, gorgeous, and all his.

"You really think I would cheat on you?" Lyla demanded, voice rising in the small space.

"Don't test me, Lyla."

"You are such an idiot!"

"I'm an idiot for noticing your fascination with each other?"

"If you weren't such a blind prick, you would've noticed that our fascination wasn't for each other but a mutual caring for your company. I came by today because I've been going stir-crazy. I've been on the road for over a year. In Maine, I had a full-time job. It's all well and good to go out with Carmen and Aunt Isabel, but I need something to get my mind off the past."

"I don't want you to get a job."

"Why?"

He didn't know how to put into words how he felt because everything he wanted to say was downright selfish.

"Why?" Lyla persisted and jabbed him in the arm. "Because you want me at your beck and call?"

"I don't want you to have to quit a job when you get pregnant." That sounded like the least selfish thing to say.

"And if I never get pregnant?"

His hands tightened on the wheel. "Lyla, I run a company. When I come home, I want you there. I don't want you working a different schedule from me where we never get to see each other and you're exhausted."

"But I need to do something, and I love your company. If we'd never dated, I would still be working there."

"Dad taught you a lot in a short amount of time." That much was obvious.

"Yes. I want to go to the opening of Incognito. Have there been other parties you've turned down because you think I don't want to go?"

"Yes and no. I'd rather be at home with you."

"I think it'll be good for us to go out. I'll have Carmen come too."

He ground his teeth. Not only would he have to keep an eye on Lyla, but he also had to watch out for Carmen, and she was unpredictable.

"If you won't let me work, then I'm going to volunteer with Alice for outreach."

That was something he couldn't object to. If he tried to stop her, she might accept a job from Marcus and that couldn't happen. "That will make Janice happy. I believe Alice has a project every month, but you don't need to attend every one."

Lyla circled back to her earlier question. "Do you really think I would cheat on you?"

She hadn't done anything to deserve his accusation. He was the one who had been unfaithful. He feared she would find someone kind, gentle, and normal. He honestly didn't know what she saw in him. "No, I know you wouldn't."

"Then why accuse me of that?"

He was going to sound like an asshole. There was no getting around that. "I'm selfish."

"I know," she said.

He let out a long breath, trying to brush off his jealousy. "I've always had you to myself. I like it like that. Marcus is closer to your age and you two hit it off so easily... I don't like seeing any man close to you."

Lyla said nothing, and his heart began to pound. Had he just eradicated the past four months with foolish words?

"I'm sorry," he said as he exited the freeway. "I'm fucked up. When it comes to you, my emotions are all over the place. I'm still trying to adjust to having you here. I want you to be happy, but I also want to be the center of your world. I know that's messed up, but it's how I am."

He glanced at her, but the fall of her hair concealed her expression.

"Lyla?"

No answer.

"I'm going to try to rein it in. If you want to volunteer with outreach, that's fine."

Still no response.

"If you need more things to keep you busy, maybe you can work with me." He floored the gas pedal so they could get home faster, and he could see just how badly he was fucking this up. "I haven't been trying to hide you away; I've been trying to give you time to recover. Me too. It's not easy going into work and acting like everything's okay. Sometimes I pick up the phone before I realize Vinny's not going to pick up the other end. Knowing I can't call my dad is even worse. The only bright spot in my life is you, and I need access to you all the time. That makes me greedy and selfish. I don't want to share you with anyone. I want your whole focus on me when I come home. But I realize you do need more, and I'm going to have to adjust to that. Yes, I watch you on the home security cameras. Not because I think you're doing something wrong. I need to see for myself that you're okay. Knowing the man who murdered Dad and hurt you is still out there will always make me paranoid."

Gavin turned into the driveway of their home and turned to her.

"Look at me," he said.

Lyla turned her silver blue eyes on him and his stomach clenched with want.

"I'm sorry."

She shook her head.

"What?"

"I like the way Marcus, Alice, and Janice looked at me today. They didn't see me as a victim or in recovery. They just saw me for me and that felt good. It made me feel normal. Marcus liked my ideas, and Alice was ecstatic that I wanted to help her with outreach. I need to be needed too, Gavin."

"I understand that." His need for her would only go so far. She needed to have a life. At least she would be working for Pyre Casinos. He should be thankful for that.

"I think Marcus is hot."

His need to make amends flew out the window. *"What?"*

Lyla grinned mischievously. "I can admire his looks without being interested in him sexually."

"No, you can't." He reached for her and hauled her over the console. "You're not allowed to think that any man is remotely attractive. I can't take it."

"I belong to you, Gavin."

That didn't reassure him.

"I won't leave you, and I think you're the hottest man I've ever seen. I love you. You're a great man, and you're mine." She pressed a chaste kiss on his lips. "Now, go back to work, and when you come home, you'll make it up to me."

Gavin's heart was in his throat as she got out of the car and sashayed slowly to the front door.

9

LYLA

"STOP, GAVIN."

"I don't like this," he said for the eighth time in an hour.

Lyla eyed her possessive husband who looked amazing in a tux. He freaked out when he saw what she was wearing —a crisscross black halter dress with a row of diamonds low on her back and stilettos. She and Carmen had their hair done at the salon, and then Carmen did her makeup. She enjoyed Gavin's stupefied look when she posed for him. He made love to her twice and begged her to change into another dress, but she held firm. She had to repair both her makeup and hair while he changed.

He'd been moody ever since she had lunch with Marcus, Janice, and Alice, but he didn't object when Alice asked if she would be interested in volunteering at a local dog shelter. She told Carmen about it, and she was down to help. She understood Gavin's need for control, but she wouldn't let it dictate her life. She needed something to keep her occupied. Being able to help others through the Pyre Foundation seemed like a win-win.

"I don't want you out of my sight," Gavin said.

"I know," she said.

"Blade and the others will be there as well."

She didn't complain since his concern for her safety wasn't unfounded. She had been kidnapped and attacked by a killer who'd carved her up like a turkey on Thanksgiving. He wouldn't allow it to happen again. This event was giving Manny's killer an opening if he wanted to finish the job. She almost backed out, but stubbornness forced her to attend. She couldn't hide forever, and this was good publicity for the casino and Gavin's image. There were more pros than cons so, despite his bitching, here they were.

She took his hand. "It's going to be fine."

Gavin didn't answer, but he squeezed her hand. She looked out at the colorful Strip as the SUV crawled through traffic. It was Friday night in Las Vegas, and The Strip was pumping with people looking for a good time.

The SUV pulled up to one of the Pyre Casinos. Gavin opened the door and helped her out. Janice prepped her for the press coverage, but she underestimated the noise and size of the crowd. Reporters called out their names and begged for pictures. Janice appeared out of nowhere and told them where to stand to be photographed. Lyla had attended many of these in her younger days, but she and Gavin had both changed since then. Her anxiety skyrocketed, and her palms were damp with sweat. She instantly regretted coming and felt exposed and uncomfortable.

"I love you," Gavin said.

Distracted, she looked up as the click of cameras echoed around them. "What?"

"I love you," he said as if his staff, the press, and a ridiculous amount of people begging to explore a new Pyre nightclub didn't surround them.

"I love you too," she said.

He raised her hand to his lips and kissed her palm. The paparazzi went nuts, and Lyla was nearly blinded by camera flashes.

"Dad would be proud of you for forcing me to come out for this," Gavin said.

Lyla smiled up at him. "He loved these events."

He grunted. "He thrived on the energy. I used to and now I don't know."

Lyla placed her hand on his chest and smiled for the cameras so they could move on. "We're different people now. We don't have to attend every opening, but we should go every now and then."

"Great, amazing!" Janice said and ushered them into the club. "Thank you for bringing him, Lyla," she said in a low undertone before she addressed Gavin. "We have Ricky Mars and his band playing for three hours, and two other hot artists going on after him. We have ten celebrities, one at each VIP table. Athletes, singers, movie stars. We only have room for about a quarter of the people waiting outside, but there's always tomorrow night. We're giving masks at the door. This is Incognito, after all."

"Are we going for kinky?" Gavin asked.

"It's an added layer of mystery to keep the libido going. The celebrities are going to wear their masks unless they're taking pictures, of course. Please stay at least two hours. Looks like we'll be wrapping this up around five," Janice said.

"In the morning?" Lyla asked.

Janice winked. "If I'm lucky. I have a table reserved for you, but you should circulate, Gavin. A lot of heavy hitters are here tonight. I know Marcus has a list of people he wants you to meet, so you might want to hook up with him to discuss. Gotta go. Enjoy and here are your masks."

Lyla took her mask, which was made of elaborate black lace with diamonds framing her eyes. Gavin had a black mask that was very *Phantom of the Opera*. It covered his eyes and half of his face. Lyla froze when he donned the mask. Even though she knew it was him, a part of her went cold with fear, remembering Manny's murderer's mask.

"Here," Gavin said and took the strip of lace from her cold fingers and tied the ribbon in the back of her head to secure it. "I'm getting too old for this shit, but we'll do it to make Janice happy."

Lyla shook herself as Gavin led her through the nightclub, which had a very different vibe to it than Lux or The Room. Incognito had two levels. From the second level, she could see the whole club. Sweeping staircases gave the club a Renaissance flair. The seductive crimson light invited one to indulge in dark fantasies. The furniture was unrelieved black, as were the walls. Large mirrors on the walls reflected the light and projected images of people writhing on the dance floor. The undercurrent of sexuality in this club ensured it would be a success. The bartenders and servers wore leather and lace uniforms and masks that enhanced their features. The staff was amped and ready to go.

"What do you think?" Gavin asked.

"There is gonna be a lot of sex in this club," she said wryly.

He laughed. "If they have the stamp from the club, they get a discount on a room in the hotel. Let's hope people want a full one-night stand instead of a quickie."

"This *is* Sin City."

"You gotta love it," he said and put an arm around her as he led her down the staircase.

Staff inclined their heads to them as a woman wearing head to toe leather escorted them to their private table, which was already occupied. It took Lyla a moment to recognize Carmen in her skintight leather pants, sky-high heels, and a lace bustier that bared two inches of her flat, toned stomach. Her white lace mask had ruby-colored stones surrounding her blue eyes. Gavin stopped and cursed under his breath. Lyla rushed to Carmen and threw her arms around her.

"You look great!"

"You too," Carmen said and gave her ass a sharp smack.

"Carmen," Gavin said, voice tight.

Carmen gave him a cool look. "Gavin."

"Don't get into trouble tonight, Carmen."

Carmen stiffened and put her hands on her hips. "Excuse me?"

"You look like—"

Lyla clapped a hand over Gavin's mouth. "You look hot, and you're going to cause a commotion. He's nervous."

Carmen flipped her hair and fixed her boobs in her top. "He should be."

Gavin yanked her hand from his mouth. "I just want to get through tonight without drama. Got me?"

"I'm not making any promises," Carmen said.

"Gavin?" Marcus joined their group, wearing a dashing cape and scarlet shirt with his tux. He wore a red mask identical to Gavin's. He kissed Lyla on the cheek and smiled at her. "You look great." His eyes moved to Carmen. "I don't think we've met."

"This is Vinny's widow, Carmen," Gavin said.

Marcus took Carmen's hand and kissed her knuckles. "My condolences."

Carmen gave Gavin a steely look before she focused on Marcus. "Thank you. And you are?"

"Marcus. I'm the new COO."

Carmen's lips pursed, and she withdrew her hand. "Vinny's replacement. Nice to meet you. You finished Incognito. It looks great."

Marcus's eyes were intense behind his mask. "I'd like to talk to you, if you don't mind."

Gavin stiffened, but Lyla kept her gaze on Carmen who looked surprised.

"I'm here to have fun and keep Lyla company. I don't want to discuss my husband," Carmen said.

"We don't have to discuss him. We can talk about something else," Marcus said.

"Marcus, can I talk to you?" Gavin said abruptly.

"Sure." Marcus nodded to Carmen. "I'll look for you later."

As Gavin led Marcus away, Carmen voiced what Lyla was thinking.

"For what?"

"Marcus is blunt and a bit strange, but I like him," Lyla said.

"But why would he want to talk to me? As Gavin said, I'm just a *widow*," Carmen said bitterly. "As if that's all I am, a dead man's wife. Jesus, I'm a person, damn it."

"You know Gavin has no tact," she said consolingly.

"And no manners."

"Let's get a drink," she said and led Carmen to the bar.

Carmen took care of ordering drinks and was in the middle of asking the bartender where she got her boob job when Lyla heard someone say her name. Alice wore an unflattering satin dress reminiscent of a 70's prom dress. The community outreach coordinator had absolutely no fashion sense and was clearly out of her element in a club.

Lyla gave Alice a hug and turned to Carmen and the bartender who were feeling each other's boobs. Lyla cleared her throat, and when that didn't get Carmen's attention, she gave her cousin a solid kick in the butt.

"Carmen, this is Alice, the community outreach coordinator. Alice, this is my cousin, Carmen. She's coming with us to the dog shelter next week to volunteer," Lyla said.

"Nice to meet you." Carmen looked Alice up and down with a frown, clearly disturbed by her appearance. "You work for Pyre Casinos?"

"Yes. I just moved from Utah," Alice said uneasily.

"Mormon?" Carmen asked.

"No. Why?"

"Just wondering."

Lyla gave Carmen a quelling glance before she turned back to Alice. "I'm really looking forward to volunteering. I like dogs. I've always wanted one, but my parents wouldn't let me have one."

"And now?" Alice asked.

"Now?" Lyla asked blankly.

"You can get one now."

Lyla was struck by the notion. "Um, I don't know."

"Since the recession, hundreds of dogs have been abandoned. Each shelter is filled to the max," Alice said.

"Does Gavin even like dogs?" Carmen asked as she handed her a pink drink.

"No idea."

"Oh, gosh, um, maybe adopting a dog isn't the best idea," Alice said, wringing her hands.

"How long have you been working at Pyre Casinos?" Carmen asked.

"A year. My position was created after..." Alice flushed and looked away.

"After Gavin went to jail and my husband and Manny Pyre were murdered?" Carmen asked.

"Oh, my gosh, I'm so sorry," Alice said and pressed a hand to her chest.

"It's okay, Alice," Lyla said, squeezing her hand. "I'm glad your position was created. It's great that Pyre Casinos created the Pyre Foundation and are giving back to the community."

"Yes," Alice said, clearly relieved. "Mr. Pyre has given me free rein, really. I'm so excited that I get to make a difference through his generosity."

She liked Alice's earnest, down to earth personality. There were far too few of her type in Las Vegas, the land of sex, money, and superficiality. Carmen watched Alice carefully as if she couldn't figure her out. On the surface, Carmen and Alice had nothing in common.

"Here come the masses," Lyla said as the VIPs came down the staircase with their entourages and a swarm of paparazzi.

"Kody Singer's here?" Carmen snapped.

"The movie star?" Alice asked, going on tiptoe to get a better look.

"He'd better not come by me," Carmen said.

"Why?" Alice asked.

"He used to drunk call me all the time, that asshole. It used to piss Vinny off."

Alice's mouth dropped. "You used to date...?"

"He was a weeklong fling when Vinny and I were on a break," Carmen said with a one-shoulder shrug.

"She broke his heart," Lyla said. "Kody is a pretty nice guy for a movie star." Carmen let out a rude snort. "Come on, Carmen, he was really romantic."

"He doesn't know how to take no for an answer," Carmen said sourly and spotted the next celeb. "Douchebag in the house! Carter Raymond is here. Seriously, when's the last time he even played football? What a fucking showoff."

"You know him personally?" Alice asked.

"When your husband is the COO of Pyre Casinos, you're obliged to go to a lot of events. You meet people," Carmen said offhandedly.

"You stay around long enough, you'll know celebrities personally," Lyla said, recognizing Jennifer Kingsley, a movie actress who thought she was God's gift to the world. Yes, Janice invited some bigshot VIPs who would draw a huge crowd.

"Me? Celebrities?" Alice let out a nervous giggle-snort. "I don't think so."

Carmen signaled to the bartender for another drink. "If you get celebrities involved in your community projects, it would be great publicity."

"I'm having a hard time recruiting volunteers, much less a celebrity."

Carmen looked thoughtful as she downed another drink. "I'll see what I can do."

"W-what?" Alice asked, but Carmen had already disappeared into the crowd.

"Come, let's go to our table," Lyla said.

"Table?"

"Janice reserved a table for us," Lyla said and took her hand.

"I don't think I'm invited. That's for Mr. Pyre and—"

"And I'm his wife, and I say you're invited," she said and began to pull her through the crowd.

The music was pumping, and an excited buzz was in the air. She noticed Janice flitting through the crowd, no doubt making sure the photographers got enough shots. Halfway across the dance floor, Blade appeared out of nowhere and cleared a path. She gripped the back of his jacket and refused to release Alice who came up with a dozen excuses why she shouldn't be at her boss's table.

"Hi, who are you?" Alice asked Blade when he helped her into the booth.

"I'm Lyla's bodyguard."

"Bodyguard?" Alice echoed, eyes wide. "Are you in danger because of... before?"

"Gavin's cautious," Lyla said and looked out over the club. "Will you look at that?"

The dance floor was at full capacity. People were dancing on the staircases and any place there was room. It was like a flash mob of exotic people. Drinks were flowing and the compulsive beat urged people to move. A haze of seduction hung in the air.

"I prefer my work to this," Alice said nervously. "This is the first club I've been to in my life. I don't even know what I'm supposed to do."

"Do?" Lyla asked without taking her eyes off the dancers.

"I'm supposed to get a drink and... what?"

"Dance," Lyla said.

"Where? There's no room."

"There's always room to dance," Lyla said and winked at her. "Clubs are a fantasy, a place where people can forget their woes and flirt with a sexy stranger."

Alice eyed her uncertainly. "I don't see the appeal."

Lyla grinned. "Some people don't, but people come to Vegas to indulge in their fantasies. Come."

Impulsively, she reached for Alice's hand and pulled her out of the booth. Blade sighed but led them to the dance floor and stood nearby like a statue. Lyla felt a twinge of shame as she pulled Alice back against her and felt the other woman go rigid. Had Alice never danced or partied in her life? Everyone had to let go sometime. That was why she was here, after all. She came out tonight so her brain could shut off and she could just *be*.

"Listen to the beat," Lyla said and moved her hips.

Alice tried to copy, but her movements were stiff and awkward. Lyla kept it up until Carmen materialized with a hot man wrapped around her. His hands moving greedily over her body. Lyla felt a shaft of pain course through her at seeing Carmen with a stranger. It was inevitable that Carmen would move on, but it felt so wrong. Lyla buried her face in Alice's hair so she didn't have to witness Carmen losing herself in another man to drown out her grief. Alice stopped moving and gawked at Carmen, who was clearly trying to drive her companion insane.

Lyla glanced around at the constantly shifting crowd. A man stood on the sideline, watching the dancers. He stood mostly in shadow, but the intensity emanating from him snagged her attention before she registered who he was. Eli was a cop who approached Gavin at Lux because some thugs had beat his mother into a coma. One of her kidnappers had also participated in the attack on Eli's mother, and Eli had killed the thug before Gavin could. Was he still on the police force? Unlike the first time she saw him, Eli was dressed all in sleek black. As if he sensed her regard, he turned his head and met her gaze through the throng. She wasn't sure whether Eli was a good or bad guy and wasn't willing to take any chances. She caught Blade's eye. He immediately muscled his way toward her.

"Eli," she shouted.

Blade searched the crowd. "Where?"

"He's there—" Lyla began and stopped when she saw that he was gone. "He was right there."

"And he saw you?" Blade demanded.

"Yes. We made eye contact." Lyla released Alice, who was now moving to the beat on her own. "Is he good?"

Blade sneered. "Eli went off the rails after his mom was attacked. He quit the force, went on a bloody rampage, and disappeared off the grid."

Her heart skipped a beat. "You mean no one's seen him until now?"

"Gavin has unfinished business with Eli, but we thought he'd been killed while he was chasing down the gang members who targeted his mother."

"Why did they attack his mom?"

"He was scheduled to testify in court against a powerful drug lord. Gavin didn't hear about the hit on his mother until it was too late."

Lyla searched the dancers, but it was impossible to find anyone in the crush. She edged closer to Blade. "So...?"

Blade brushed a hand over his weapon. "So we keep our eyes open. I'll let Gavin know."

Marcus appeared at her side, eyes narrowed on Carmen and her horny companion. He walked up to Carmen and her partner who stopped their bump and grind. Carmen's mouth dropped open, and the guy backed away with his hands up. Marcus tried to pull Carmen off the dance floor, but she shoved him away. Carmen pulled Alice into the crowd, leaving Marcus behind, looking irritated.

Hard hands circled Lyla's waist. She jumped as Gavin pulled her back against him.

"I've been looking for you," Gavin said in her ear. "I want to show you the private rooms."

"Gavin," Blade said.

Gavin leaned toward him, and Blade spoke. Lyla witnessed the change in Gavin as he glanced around and then swept her under his arm and carried her off the dance floor. He pulled her through the crowd to a room manned by two security guards. Blade waited outside as Gavin waved a key card over the lock. He pulled her into a dimly lit room with a stripper pole, black loveseat, and floor-to-ceiling window that looked out at the club. It took Lyla a moment to realize that she was looking through one of the large mirrors mounted on the wall.

"Can they see us?" Lyla asked.

Couples were making out, drinking, and laughing at tables on the other side of the glass. She could see the dance floor from here and the music penetrated through the walls and kept her blood fizzing.

"There are about ten of these hidden rooms. Each one is different," Gavin said. "Are you okay?"

"Because of Eli?"

"Yes."

"I'm a little creeped, but I don't think he was looking for me."

"What makes you say that?"

"He was searching the crowd. He felt me looking at him, and then I called Blade."

"He used to grease the wheels in the police department for me. He's always been dependable, but now he's a loose cannon. I don't know his agenda."

"We shouldn't worry about it. We should just enjoy tonight."

She saw the hunger in his eyes and knew they were going to use this room for what it had been designed for. She gave him a small shove. He sat on the couch and tried to draw her on his lap, but she sauntered toward the stripper pole. She stepped onto the platform and ran her hand down the pole. Gavin was as still as a mannequin and barely breathing.

"Carmen and I have taken a lot of classes, but I don't think you've ever seen me on a stripper pole, have you?" she asked.

He cleared his throat. "No."

"Hmm." Lyla stroked the pole slowly and then walked around it, dragging her stilettos and shifting her hips seductively. She did a slow spin, feet completely off the ground, letting her body weight swing her around the pole before she stopped in front of Gavin, legs spread wide, the slit in her dress riding high on her hip. She dropped into the splits and rocked her body forward, arching her back.

"Jesus Christ!" Gavin shouted and shot up from the couch.

"You're supposed to watch, not touch," she chastised as her gaze went past him to the people less than six feet away, completely unaware of what she was doing on the other side of the mirror.

"If you think I can watch while you dance, you're out of your mind," he growled.

"Sit, Gavin, and let me dance for you," she said.

His crotch was tented. She knew he was already gone, but she wanted to do this. A sultry beat slipped through the walls. Gavin didn't go back to the couch. He stood less than two feet away, hungry eyes fixed on her.

Lyla stood in front of the pole, hands above her head and slowly, very slowly sank down. She could hear Gavin's ragged breathing over the music, and watched as his hand went to his crotch and gripped hard. The tendons on his neck stood out, and she knew he wasn't going to last. Taking pity on him, Lyla went on her hands and knees and stuck her butt out as she rose. Gavin cursed and grabbed her.

Lyla laughed as he positioned her on her knees on the couch, facing the club. She felt cold air on her ass as he shifted her dress up and then his fingers slid into her. She moaned and then clapped her hand over her mouth as a man leaned toward the mirror to fix his hair. He was a foot away, staring right at her, and Gavin was about to fuck her.

"Gavin," she said and tried to wriggle away.

"He can't see you," Gavin said in her ear as he slid inside her in one firm push that sheathed him to the hilt.

"B-but, I can't!" she said, scandalized as a woman joined the man. She panted like a bitch in heat. "Oh, my God, Gavin!"

"People get off on this shit, fucking in public," Gavin said, slipping his hand into her dress and squeezing her breast. "I wouldn't mind fucking you in front of an audience. I want everyone to know you belong to me. Only I *ever* get to fuck you."

"I thought that was what the ring was for." She squirmed beneath him, not caring about the congregation of girls in front of her who were putting on lip-gloss and fixing their tits. As he thrust slowly, torturously, she began to lose all inhibitions. Who cared if only a mirror separated her from hundreds of people? Her man was making love to her. Nothing else mattered.

"The ring isn't enough. Nothing is," Gavin said into her ear and sped up his thrusts. "I can't stand having other people look at you, having you smile at others. I want it all for myself."

"You're the one who's in me," Lyla said as he collared her throat.

"I'm the only one, *ever*."

She touched herself as Gavin brought it home. She braced her hands on the fogged-up glass as she panted and writhed against it before she went limp. A young woman came up to the glass and checked out her ass before she winked at herself and disappeared into the crowd.

"I needed my fix," Gavin said as he pulled out and trailed kisses down her spine. "This damn dress."

Lyla shuddered and sat back on her heels, trembling. "Do you think this will ever ease up?"

"I can't imagine it." He nuzzled her face and kissed her long and sweet. "Maybe if we have a couple of kids, I'll have to rein it in..."

"You're kid crazy," she said, shaking her head.

"Have you taken a pregnancy test?"

"I had my period recently."

Gavin zipped himself up. "I'd better up my game."

"You up it anymore, and I won't be able to walk."

He drew her to her feet, cupped her face, and kissed her. "I love you, Lyla Pyre."

She let out a shaky breath. "I believe you."

"Good." He smacked her ass. "Now that you forced me to come to this, first we circulate, then we're going home to spend all weekend in bed."

Lyla ignored the guards' lecherous grins and Blade's smirk when they walked out. She went to the mirror to make sure she looked presentable and that no one could see inside. She was lazy-eyed, lipstick smeared and hair mussed, but otherwise perfectly presentable for a nightclub. Her eyes glittered through the slits in the mask.

They circulated to the VIP tables where Gavin caught up with acquaintances, asked about their accommodations, and got feedback on the club. Some of the celebrities asked outright about Manny and his murder. Gavin told the truth —that whoever did it hadn't been apprehended. He introduced her as his wife. People looked at them curiously or with a knowing smirk as if they knew that they had just fucked. Gavin's hands were constantly moving over her ass, bare back, or belly. Kody Singer was the only one stupid enough to try to draw her away from Gavin, and it was probably to ask about Carmen. Gavin had him in a headlock before Kody could say two words to her.

"You don't touch or talk to my wife," Gavin ordered.

There were flashes from the paparazzi as they honed in on the commotion. When Gavin showed no signs of releasing Kody, Lyla punched him in the shoulder.

"I know him, Gavin!" she shouted.

Gavin turned to her, wrenching poor Kody's neck. "How the fuck do you know him?"

She heard Kody choking and punched him again. "I know him because of Carmen. Let him go!"

Gavin released Kody as Janice appeared. Janice looked from the gagging movie star to the paparazzi and then Gavin who was as composed as ever.

"What happened?" Janice demanded while she tried to shoo away the paparazzi.

"Misunderstanding," Gavin said as he clapped Kody on the back. "You're okay, right?"

Kody wore a terrified expression until he noticed the paparazzi. He was an A-list movie star for a reason. His face smoothed into a world-class smile, and the paparazzi lowered their cameras, clearly disappointed. As soon as Janice shooed the paparazzi away, Kody jerked away from Gavin as though he were a serial killer. Lyla tried to make amends, but Kody backed away as if she had a contagious disease.

"He's my husband," Lyla told Kody in an apologetic tone.

"We're leaving," Gavin decreed and dragged her out of the club.

"God, you're such a psycho," Lyla grumbled while Blade

followed, chuckling. "You can't kill someone for talking to me."

"Did that asshole *not* see my hands on you? My ring on your finger?" Gavin growled.

"He wanted to talk to me to get info on Carmen."

Gavin boosted her into the back of the SUV and got in beside her.

"First Marcus and now that asshole. What the fuck? Carmen just lost her husband. Maybe it's the way she's dressed," Gavin said sourly.

"What about Marcus? He's interested in her?"

"I don't know what he is. I told him to lay off, and he told me to butt out of it."

"He told you that?" *Go, Marcus*, she thought.

Gavin ran a hand through his hair. "The freaking world is tilting sideways. Shit."

10

LYLA

"You're so beautiful."

A man in a black suit and white mask hovered over her. He brushed his gloved thumb, slick with some warm liquid over her lips. The iron tang of blood touched her tongue. She tried to spit it out, but the man clamped a hand over her mouth. She gagged as Manny's blood slid down her throat. Fathomless black eyes stared at her through the slits in the mask.

"It's a shame I have to do this to you. You're at the wrong place at the wrong time, baby."

She saw the glint of metal out of the corner of her eye and knew what was coming. No matter how hard she fought, she couldn't defend herself. Pain ripped through her abdomen as the knife sliced through skin and muscle. She felt a gush of blood, and then her attacker slashed down again and again and again. There was no reprieve.

Lyla screamed and sat up in bed, fingers curled into claws as she tried to gouge out the eyes of the crime lord. She stared at her surroundings through a haze of tears before she realized she wasn't in Manny's mansion but the master suite of her home with Gavin. She rocked back and forth, trying to banish the vivid memories of the attack and the taste of Manny's blood. She was shaking uncontrollably and covered in a layer of cold sweat. The memories came without warning, slamming into her with such force that she curled into a protective ball.

She was grateful Gavin was already gone for the day. A text from Carmen drew her out of the past and into the present. Today, she was supposed to help Alice at the dog shelter. She didn't want to leave the house, but Gavin would know something was wrong if she didn't go. She forced herself to dress, put on makeup, and go downstairs.

"Lyla," Blade said and gestured to the waiting SUV.

"I want to drive myself," she said, glad for the shield of sunglasses. Her eyes were still a little swollen. Blade would have reported that small detail to Gavin.

Blade hesitated and then, "Security-wise, this is the safer choice."

She held up the keys to Gavin's Aston Martin. "Can you have one of the guys bring the car around?"

"Lyla..."

"Blade, not today," she said shortly.

Blade tossed the keys to one of the men and pulled out his phone. She scowled as he spoke to Gavin.

"Lyla wants to drive herself," Blade said without preamble and then extended the phone to her.

Lyla snatched it. "I'm driving myself."

"Why?" Gavin asked.

"Because I want to."

"It's safer to—"

"I need some space today, Gavin," she said, and her voice shook.

"What's wrong?"

"Nothing. I just want to drive myself."

Gavin didn't say anything for a moment and then said, "Give the phone back to Blade."

She did as she was told and hurried to the Aston Martin. The guard blinked when she got behind the wheel. Blade rushed to an SUV and got into the driver's seat. She blew out a breath. Gavin wasn't going to push the issue, thank God.

Two SUVs flanked her as she made her way to Aunt Isabel's house. After she parked in the driveway, she went in and chatted with her aunt before Carmen came downstairs in Uggs, ripped designer jeans, and a crop top.

"Why are you driving yourself?" Carmen asked when they walked outside.

"Because I feel like it," she snapped.

Carmen's brows went up. "What's up with you?"

"Bad dreams." Lyla rolled her shoulders to relieve the itch between her shoulder blades as she turned the key in the ignition.

"Are you fighting with Gavin?"

"No."

"Is it because he was a prick at Incognito?"

Lyla glanced at Carmen as she backed out of the driveway. "No. Why?"

"Gavin and Kody were all over the papers."

"That's your fault," Lyla said sourly. "I think Kody wanted to ask me about you. Gavin got pissed when he tried to pull me to the side."

"I'm telling you, Kody's an idiot."

"What about you?"

Carmen laughed. "Alice turned out to be good company after five shots."

"What? Carmen, you didn't corrupt her, did you?"

"Just a little bit. I took care of her when she puked her guts out. Alice couldn't go in to work the next day and vowed never to party with me again. Can we get coffee?"

Lyla navigated through the neighborhood and rolled her eyes when Blade changed lanes, nearly running someone off the road.

"Poor Alice. What kind of coffee do you want?" Lyla asked as she pulled up to a Starbucks drive-through.

"Get me a triple tall latte and a maple scone. What do you want?"

"Nothing."

"Are you sick?"

"No." She sucked in a fortifying breath and shoved down the tears just beneath the surface. "I'm just bitchy, and nothing tastes good."

Carmen hummed happily as she drank coffee and nibbled on her scone. Lyla followed the GPS instructions to the dog shelter and found a bus of casino workers in front along with Alice and a photographer. Everyone wore bright orange T-shirts with the Pyre Casino logo. Alice clapped her hands as Lyla approached and gave Carmen a frosty smile before she introduced them to the other volunteers. A low murmur of surprise rumbled through the crowd when Alice introduced her as Gavin's wife. Blade and the other guards joined the group and were forced to wear matching T-shirts. Alice gave a rundown of tasks they were going to do, which included baths, cleaning kennels, and walking the dogs.

"This place looks like a prison," Carmen said under her breath.

Lyla agreed as a staff member led them through the

building. Her heart wrenched as dogs pressed against their cages, yipping and crying out for attention. She stopped and pressed her hands against a gate. A large gray pit bull went up on its hind legs and licked her hand.

"Hi, boy," she whispered. "You're gorgeous."

"Gavin might get a new bed buddy," Carmen said with a wicked grin.

Lyla forced herself to walk away from the pit bull named Beau and finished the tour of the dog shelter. She opted to walk the dogs while Carmen decided to help at the bathing station. The first dog she took out of a cage was a small Yorkie that barked at the other dogs as he pranced by. She actually found the walking path soothing, but the Yorkie didn't have the stamina to make it halfway along the trail. She carried the dog back to the kennel and made a mark on the dog's sheet to let the other staff know she had walked him. She walked dog after dog but didn't seem to be getting anywhere. There were too many dogs and not enough volunteers. It warmed her heart to see Blade cleaning the kennels. He didn't have to participate but did so because he was a good guy. That made her feel like a bitch since she threw a fit this morning and made his job difficult.

Hours passed. When everyone else took a break to eat lunch, she made her way over to Beau. She talked to the pit bull until he calmed down. She scratched him behind the ears and smiled when he closed his eyes in delight. She opened the kennel, and even though Beau pulled at his leash, he eased up once they were outside. He sniffed the air and hopped playfully before he fell into step beside her.

She could relate to Beau's joy at being out of his cage. She was slowly learning how to live again. These aban-doned dogs hoped someone would take them home. They needed a second chance, like her. Flashbacks hit her at the strangest times. She could be swimming or watching TV, and all of a sudden, she would be covered in cold sweat, unable to breathe as she remembered being stabbed or the sound of Manny's tortured screams. Carmen reassured her that the panic attacks were normal, considering all she'd been through. She didn't want to tell Gavin because there was nothing he could do and he had his own demons to battle.

Lyla glanced down at Beau and wondered what his story was. Had he been abused or had his family decided they couldn't take care of him? Maybe he'd been found on the side of the road? Beau trotted along, marking shrubs and trees as they went. No matter what happened in his past, it wasn't stopping him from enjoying the moment. She tipped her head up to the sun, took a deep breath, and everything went black.

Something wet and slimy slid over her face. Lyla turned her face to the side and moaned. She heard a scream, and then the sound of someone running over gravel. She shielded her eyes against the sunlight and blinked at Beau who stood over her, tongue lolling. She grimaced when she caught a whiff of his doggy breath.

"Oh, my God! What happened? Did the dog attack you? Mr. Pyre is going to kill me!" Alice shouted as she grabbed Beau's leash and pulled him away from Lyla, who lay flat on her back on the walking path.

"He didn't attack me. I think I passed out," she said and put a hand to her forehead as she sat up. She dropped her face between her knees and tried to think straight.

"Did you take a break?" Alice asked.

"No."

"Oh my God, I overworked the CEO's wife," Alice said, wringing her hands.

"No, I'm fine. I'm just not feeling like myself today. I wanted to walk Beau before I got a drink."

"Phil! Phil! Come over here, will ya? She fainted!" Alice said, bouncing up and down in well-used sneakers.

An attractive man wearing worn jeans and a gray T-shirt ambled over. He pet the dog before he hunkered down beside her. Phil fixed her with an unsettling, piercing look.

"How ya feeling?" Phil asked.

"Crappy," Lyla admitted.

"This heat isn't helping," he said and hauled her up.

Lyla swayed on her feet and tried to blink away the black spots marring her vision. Phil tightened his hold.

"Come, let's get you in air conditioning," he said and helped her inside.

Alice followed with Beau who nudged the back of Lyla's leg as if he were worried about her. Alice led Beau back to his kennel. Lyla silently promised Beau that she'd come back and give him a decent walk. It wasn't his fault that she fainted on the path. Shit. How long would it be before he saw daylight?

Phil led her to an office not much bigger than a closet with pictures of dogs and cats covering the walls. He uncapped a water bottle and handed it to her. She took a healthy gulp.

"Here."

Phil held out a handful of Wheat Thins. Under normal circumstances, she wouldn't take crackers from his questionably clean hands, but she was desperate. She nodded in thanks, and once she began to munch, instantly began to feel better. Phil gave her that direct look again.

"What?" Lyla asked defensively.

"People don't just pass out. It's not *that* hot."

"I know. I've been feeling strange all day."

Phil cocked his head to the side. "Are you pregnant?"

Even as her body went cold, she shook her head. "No."

"How do you know?"

She glared at him. "Why do you want to know?"

"I don't want you to sue me."

"What?"

"I run this place. Volunteers passing out aren't good advertisement."

"Oh. Well, I'm fine now." But she didn't get up because her legs were still trembling.

"Maybe you should go to the hospital."

"No."

"I insist. If you're not pregnant, it could be something else. You don't want to take chances. Plus, you look like shit."

Before she could respond to that, Carmen appeared in the doorway. Her cousin looked as if she'd been in a wet T-shirt contest. Her crop top was nearly transparent, her jeans were covered in fur, and her Uggs squelched with each step. Phil perked up.

"I heard you fainted," Carmen said. "Are you sick?"

"I'm not sick; I just feel queasy," she said and gave Phil a dirty look.

"Who are you?" Carmen asked, getting right to the point.

"I'm Phil, a vet."

Carmen raised a brow. "And you're examining Lyla?"

Apparently, Carmen thought this was hilarious because she grinned. Phil's head kicked back as if Carmen's beauty had a physical impact on him. Lyla didn't know whether to be amused or irritated.

"In your professional opinion, what's wrong with her?

You think she has fleas or she's in heat?" Carmen asked with mock seriousness.

"I assumed she was pregnant, but she says it's not possible," Phil said.

Carmen's head whipped toward Lyla. "Pregnant?"

"I'm not," Lyla said.

"What? How do you know? Are you on something?"

Lyla gave Phil a pointed look, but he didn't budge. The exotic creature in his shitty office fascinated him.

She wiped her clammy brow. "I had my period recently."

Carmen looked at Phil. "She can still spot if she's pregnant, right?"

Phil blinked. "I really don't know much about human women who are breeding."

"Right," Lyla drawled and forced herself up. "I think I'm done for the day. I'll come back to walk Beau and the others another time."

"Thanks, Doc," Carmen said and winked at Phil before she followed Lyla into the hallway. "Are you sure you're not pregnant?"

"Positive."

Carmen didn't say anything as Blade jogged up to them. He stopped, and they got a whiff of a very distinct poop smell. They both took a step back.

"What happened? Alice said you fainted," Blade said.

"I'm fine." Lyla bounced to show that she was fine and instantly regretted it when another wave of nausea hit her. "You know, I think I really need something to eat."

"Let me get you a sandwich."

She had nearly gagged when she caught a whiff of bologna earlier. "No, I need something..." She waved her hand. "Light and fresh."

"Like what?"

"Some noodle salad or something," she said, knowing she sounded nuts but not caring. She wanted some light, fluffy meal from the deli section of a supermarket. She didn't know exactly what she wanted but...

"Okay," Blade said and pulled out his phone. "I have to call Gavin."

"About me? Blade, nothing happened!"

"Do you want me to die?" Blade asked as he dialed.

"I'm—" She ground her teeth and then snatched Blade's phone before he could speak.

"Blade? What is it?" Gavin asked brusquely on the other end.

"Hey, baby," she said and slapped Blade's hand away.

"Lyla?"

"Yeah, something happened at the dog shelter and Blade's overreacting," she said and ignored Blade's glare.

"What happened?"

Lyla winced. Gavin sounded calm, but she knew better. "I'm just not feeling well, that's all. I'm fine, though. We're leaving now."

"Are you sick? Should I call the doctor?"

"No, I'm fine. Too much sun."

"You're going home?"

"I want to get something to eat first, but after that, yeah."

"Okay. I'll see you tonight."

"Okay. Love you," Lyla said and hung up. She handed the phone back to Blade. "I'm fine."

He shook his head but didn't push it. Lyla apologized to Alice, who told her to get some rest. Her first "job" and she passed out within a couple of hours. What the hell? If Gavin heard that she fainted, he would see it as a sign that she shouldn't volunteer, which was bullshit. Maybe she shouldn't have volunteered after her episode this morning.

Blade wouldn't let her drive, which was probably a good thing. He gave the Aston Martin keys to one of the guards who was going to stay to finish their tasks. Carmen was unusually quiet as they climbed into the SUV. Lyla belted herself in, leaned back, and closed her eyes. She told Blade which supermarket to go to and rolled down the windows since they were all pretty smelly.

"Before I ruined everything, how did you do bathing the dogs?" Lyla asked.

"I don't think some of those dogs have ever had baths. They fought me like crazy, but they looked fab afterward. One of the dogs howled when I tried to blow dry him. I want to go back. They need a lot of help."

"I'm sure Phil will enjoy that," Lyla said and patted Blade's shoulder. "Thanks for helping."

Blade didn't reply. He parked, and they walked into the store. Carmen grabbed a hand basket and disappeared while Lyla went to the deli and found a pasta salad. She grabbed fresh bread and some spreads while Blade grabbed something for himself. Carmen insisted on paying for everything. Lyla grabbed one of three shopping bags.

"What did you buy?" she asked.

"Odds and ends. I'll eat at your place, and one of the guys can take me home later," Carmen said.

Lyla was too busy eating her salad and ripping off a chunk of bread to care. Carmen handed her chilled green tea. Lyla was puzzled but obliged and enjoyed the cool refreshment. They carried everything into the house and ate at the table.

"Come on, you have to finish your drink," Carmen said. "You're dehydrated."

Lyla finished the drink to satisfy her cousin so she would stop fussing. Carmen chatted about the different dogs and their needs. Lyla was happy that Carmen enjoyed herself and also wanted to go back. Lyla agreed with Beau on her mind. Pit bulls had such a bad rep, but Beau was a sweetheart. While Blade and Carmen chatted, Lyla went upstairs to pee. She was startled when someone pounded on the door.

"What are you doing?" Carmen shouted.

Lyla stared at the door. "Um, I'm using the bathroom."

"Number one or number two?"

Seriously? "Why do you care?"

"Because I have to pee too."

"Go to another bathroom!"

"Why? You said you're doing number one. Just don't flush."

"What?"

"You're wasting water, and we live in the desert!" Carmen slapped her hand on the door for emphasis. "We need to conserve as much water as possible!"

Used to Carmen's outbursts and eccentricities, she opened the door to her cousin, who clapped her on the back like a bro and shut the door in her face. Lyla went downstairs and found the cook in the kitchen.

"How are you today, Mrs. Pyre?" she asked.

"I'm okay," Lyla said and backed away when she caught a whiff of steamed broccoli.

"Is something wrong?"

Lyla waved a hand in front of her face. "I don't know."

The cook stared at her. "You like broccoli, right?"

"I do normally, but... maybe I'm coming down with some kind of weird bug."

"A bug," the cook repeated flatly. "You know I can prepare anything you want. I can cook based on what you're craving. In the past, Mr. Pyre preferred that I make meals at home and deliver, but I'm not opposed to coming here if you want to request something special."

"Oh, no, I'm fine. I'm sure it'll pass."

A bloodcurdling scream rang out from the top of the stairs. Lyla took off toward the staircase with Blade on her heels. She ran to the master bathroom and found Carmen on the floor, holding something to her chest with her head bowed, rocking back and forth. What the hell? Wondering if her cousin was having a grieving episode, she got down on her knees and wrapped her arms around Carmen.

"Are you hurt?"

Carmen shook her head. Blade closed the door to give them privacy.

"What's going on?" she asked.

Carmen mumbled something incoherent.

"What? Carmen, you're scaring me."

Carmen raised her tear-streaked face. The broad grin on her face startled Lyla.

"You're pregnant," Carmen said.

Lyla's arms fell away. "What? What are you talking about?"

"I did a pregnancy test using the pee you left in the toilet."

It took a moment for her to register what Carmen was saying. When it penetrated, she fell on her ass. Her cousin held up a white wand with the word 'pregnant' on it. Lyla snatched the test and shook it as if it was an eight ball and the words would change.

"I can't be. I just had my period two weeks ago."

"I looked it up on my phone. In the beginning, you can still spot when you're pregnant."

Lyla couldn't describe the feelings rushing through her.

She leaped to her feet and jabbed the wand at her cousin. "You had no right to do this!"

Carmen stared at her. "Don't you want to know?"

Lyla paced around the bathroom, blindsided by the news. She was still trying to overcome panic attacks, bad dreams, and depression, and now she was pregnant? She stopped and shook her head. "I want to take another test."

Carmen got to her feet, watching her cautiously. "Lyla, you can't fake this kind of stuff."

"B-but I'm not ready," she stammered.

Carmen held up both hands. "Wait, do you *want* to be pregnant?"

"Yes. No. Not right now."

"But you haven't been on any birth control. You must have known this was a possibility."

Lyla ignored that. "You bought a test at the store?"

"Yes."

"Do you have another one?"

"Yes. Can you pee again?"

"That's why you gave me that green tea, isn't it?" she asked.

Carmen nodded.

Lyla didn't have to pee, so she tossed the wand in the trash and hurried downstairs with Carmen on her heels. Blade was nowhere to be found, which was a good thing, considering she wouldn't be able to conceal that something was wrong. She downed two bottles of water while Carmen pulled a bouquet out of her shopping bag and arranged them on the dining table.

Lyla couldn't stay still. She went outside to get some fresh air and paced around the pool, arms wrapped around herself. She couldn't be pregnant, could she? Yes, she hadn't taken the pills, which left her open to pregnancy, but they

had been married less than four months. What were the
chances that Gavin had super sperm? Oh, God, he would be
ecstatic. She covered her face with both hands. Gavin Pyre,
former crime lord, CEO of Pyre Casinos, husband, and
maybe baby daddy. Pregnant... Lyla felt a surge of protective-
ness, joy, and terror when she thought about the being that
could be growing in her tummy.

When she was ready for the next test, she rushed in the
house, interrupting Carmen and the cook who were deep in
conversation. The second pregnancy test was on the vanity.
Lyla was trying to read the directions when Carmen
barged in.

"Here."

Carmen took the wand out of the box, uncapped it, and
rushed her over to the toilet. "You have to pee on here," she
instructed.

Carmen obviously wasn't going anywhere, and Lyla was
feeling strangely vulnerable, so she didn't say anything.
After she peed on the stick, Carmen recapped it and set it on
the counter.

"Now we wait," Carmen said.

Lyla sat on the edge of the tub and clasped her hands
together. "Oh, my God."

Carmen sat beside her. "Aren't you excited?"

"I don't know. I knew this was a possibility, but I never
thought I would get pregnant." She couldn't take her eyes off
the innocent looking wand that would change her life.

"Have you talked about kids?"

"Yes. He wants them badly."

"Well, he is older than you are."

"Yes." She hesitated and then confided, "When he was in
jail, he had a dream about a little girl named Nora. He said

the dream was so real he could smell her, feel her weight against his chest. She gave him hope."

"Nora," Carmen said quietly. "I like it. His mother's name, right?"

She nodded. "I wanted to go on birth control, but after he told that story, I couldn't. I didn't want to take that away from him. He believes our kids will be his redemption."

"You might be making his dreams come true, but what about yours?"

"It's kind of too late, isn't it?" she asked with a hollow laugh, gesturing to the pregnancy test.

"You have choices, Lyla."

"Like what?"

Carmen pinched her. "You know how I feel about Gavin."

"Actually, I'm not sure what you think about him anymore."

Carmen straightened her shoulders. "I didn't really know Gavin when you started dating him. I just liked the fact we were cousins dating cousins. I thought that was cool. I knew Gavin loved you, and Vinny loved me. In my mind, that's all we needed. I didn't care what they did on the side as long as they came home to us. I had no idea Gavin would cheat on you. I felt just as betrayed as you did. I trusted Gavin to take care of you, to love you as your father never had, and he failed. Then he killed that man in your basement, and you begged me to help you leave. Helping you escape, knowing I may never see you again was one of the hardest things I ever had to do." Carmen let out a ragged breath. "Gavin never stopped looking for you. I didn't know if you were better off without him. I'm not going to lie. When he brought you back, I would do almost anything to make you want to stay. I'm glad Manny got involved. You've always had a strong connection with him, almost as strong as your connection with Gavin."

Lyla brushed away tears. Manny would never see his grandchild. Her child never knowing its paternal grandfather made her heart ache with grief, bitterness, and anger. Life was so unfair... and his killer was still out there. Lyla shivered.

"Manny made Gavin see reason, and Gavin began to treat you like the queen you are. Then Vinny died."

Carmen's voice was flat and emotionless. Lyla put an arm around her cousin to comfort her.

"Everything started to fall apart. Manny was murdered, and I almost lost you again." Carmen sniffled. "I'm glad you asked me to get you out of Vegas. It's what I was planning for myself, and I was glad to have a partner even though I suspected Gavin would look for you. I was right." Carmen let out a watery laugh. "God, he is one stubborn son of a bitch."

Lyla laughed and felt some of her anxiety slip away. If they could get through the murders of their loved ones, they could handle this.

"When he came for you in Montana, I couldn't read him, and that scared the crap out of me. I didn't know if he would punish you for leaving. When he forced you to marry him, I was even more alarmed. In the jet, he nearly hit me." When Lyla tried to explain, Carmen patted her hand. "I know Gavin's been through the wringer, and I know he carries a lot of guilt on his shoulders. We're all scarred by what happened, and Gavin doesn't know how to deal with losing his father and best friend. I get it. We're women, and we have each other. Gavin? He only has you. When I saw you at the funeral, I knew."

"Knew what?"

"That he had let you in all the way. His shields were down. He wasn't a coldblooded robot; he was just... Gavin. You make him human. He needs you." Carmen let out a choked sob and leaned forward, hands over her chest. "It's the way Vinny needed me. I miss him so much."

Lyla rested her head on her cousin's shoulder. They cried together, their sobs echoing in the bathroom.

"I'm happy for you and Gavin even though I think he's a shithead."

Lyla chuckled. Carmen rose and helped her to her feet. With tears trickling down her cheeks, Carmen clasped Lyla's hands and squeezed.

"Life moves on, which means we have to as well. I am *so* happy for you. I'm going to be here for you every step of the way. Everything is going to be fine. You know that, right?"

Lyla nodded, too overcome to speak.

"You ready?" Carmen asked.

She took a deep breath, and still holding hands, they walked to the vanity and peered down at the wand.

Pregnant.

Lyla's head spun. "Oh, my God."

Carmen squealed. "I'm going to be an aunty!"

"And I'm going to be a mom," she said and felt her world tilt sideways.

Carmen pushed Lyla on a bench and clapped her hands together like a cheerleader. "Okay, so I already talked to your cook. She's going to come daily to prepare meals since you're sensitive to certain foods right now. She's preparing something extra special for tonight."

"What? Why?"

"Because you have to tell Gavin, right?"

Lyla took a deep breath. "Yes."

"How do you want to tell him?"

"What do you mean?"

Carmen fetched her phone. "So on the ride home, I went on YouTube and there are all these ways women have told their husbands they're pregnant. Here, watch this one; it's so cute!"

Lyla watched a woman send her husband on a scavenger hunt, which really was cute. Carmen proceeded to show her at least eight videos of women telling their husbands they were pregnant in creative ways. Instead of being inspired, Lyla felt more nervous.

"Can't I just *tell* him?"

Carmen's face dropped. "Well, yeah, but this is your first. Don't you want it to be extra special?"

"I can't imagine telling Gavin to get a bun out of the oven or giving him a crossword that he has to figure out. That's just not us."

"Okay." Carmen pocketed her phone, clearly disappointed, but then she lit up again. "Oh, my gosh. You will not *believe* what I found at the store! It's going to be perfect!"

Carmen ran out of the bathroom. Lyla listened to the sound of her thundering downstairs while she stared at the positive pregnancy test. Her life would never be the same. Carmen came back with a pink onesie in her hands. She held it up and Lyla saw that it said, "Daddy's Princess." Lyla clapped a hand over her chest because it felt as if her heart was breaking.

"They didn't have a boy outfit, so I guess this is meant to be."

"It's perfect," Lyla choked out and hugged her cousin. "What would I do without you?"

"You'll never have to know."

"Will you be her godmother?"

Carmen burst into tears.

When Gavin walked through the front door, Lyla was relieved. Carmen had been going crazy on Pinterest for hours. Lyla was so wound up that she wanted to blurt it out the second she saw him. Instead, she ran and threw herself into his arms. Gavin gave her a deep kiss.

"You all right, baby girl?" he asked.

"I am now."

Gavin looked past her and noticed Carmen. "What happened to you?"

"This is what you look like after you give ten dogs a bath," Carmen said with a hand on her hip.

"How's your mother?" Gavin asked.

Surprised and pleased he was making an effort to be social and considerate, Lyla patted his chest.

"She cleans a lot," Carmen said with a shrug, "but her friends signed her up for salsa classes, so she's been going out more."

"Have you made any plans?"

"Like?"

"If you want to buy a house, or if you're going to stay here?"

Carmen glanced at Lyla with a mischievous twinkle in her eye. "I'm not planning to leave anytime soon."

Gavin relaxed slightly. "The RV is in a safe place. I didn't get rid of it."

"Good to know," Carmen said and eyed him. "What are your plans?"

"Excuse me?"

"What's your plan for the future?"

"To keep Lyla happy and safe," Gavin said.

Lyla glanced between the two people she loved most and

wanted to shake her head. They glared at one another as if they were adversaries.

"Bye, Carmen!" she said deliberately.

Carmen sniffed. "One of your guys is taking me home. Lyla, call me later."

Lyla waved and looked up at Gavin. "You want to shower before we eat?"

"Yeah." He cupped her face. "You sure you're okay?"

"Yes." How would he react to her news? He made it clear that he wanted her pregnant but... how would he be *after* he got her pregnant? Her enthusiasm dimmed as old insecurities crept in.

"I'll be quick," he said and kissed her. He paused and dropped his nose to her neck and inhaled. "You smell good."

"Pomegranate body wash."

"Yum."

He slapped her ass and went upstairs. Lyla paced and chewed her nails. She felt as if an expanding balloon was in her chest, and it kept growing until she couldn't breathe properly. She wouldn't be able to calm down until Gavin knew. She grabbed her wine glass, which held apple cider. She imagined it was wine and downed it in one gulp. The dining table was set with Carmen's flowers and candles. Because she had to do something, Lyla made their plates. When Gavin appeared, he took in the table setting.

"What's the occasion?" he asked.

"Your cook wanted to do something nice for us," she said and had to make an effort not to look at the gift bag on the chair.

Gavin fingered the petals of a flower. "Nice."

They sat, and he immediately dug into the meal. Lyla examined him furtively. He wasn't the same man she fell in love with as a teenager. At eighteen, how could she have prepared herself for a life with him? They had their highs and lows, and now, here they were, expectant parents. She tried to imagine Gavin holding a baby. The image tugged at her heartstrings. He was such an alpha. If he loved their baby as much as he loved her, their daughter would never want to leave home. *It might not be a girl*, she reminded herself.

"How was the dog shelter?" Gavin asked.

"Um, it was great," she said and forced herself to eat. "I want to volunteer there regularly. Carmen does too. She bathed dogs, and I took them out of their kennels and walked them on this path. There was this cute pit bull, Beau, that I walked—"

"A *what*?"

Lyla frowned. "A pit bull."

"Pit bulls are one of the most aggressive dog breeds in the world."

"He's not aggressive. He's a sweetheart. When I fainted, he just stayed with me until someone found me—" She broke off when Gavin dropped his fork. "What?"

"Did you just say you fainted?" he asked in a quiet, icy voice.

Oh, shit. "I felt a little dizzy, and I had a spell, but I'm fine now."

"Why the fuck didn't Blade take you to the hospital?"

Gavin looked murderous. Things were spinning out of control, as usual. She splayed a hand on his chest, which was hard as a rock.

"Gavin, I'm fine."

"Will you stop saying that? People don't pass out if they're fine. And you were walking a pit bull that could have mauled—"

"Gavin!" Lyla braced her hands on his shoulders. "Nothing happened."

"Something sure as fuck did happen. You lied to me," he growled.

"But I'm fine now." She jumped with her hands in the air. "See? I'm fine."

"But you fainted."

"I didn't eat. I was stupid, and it's not Blade's fault. He tried to tell you, but I took his phone. I'm sorry."

"You realize you hold my sanity in your hands?" Amber eyes probed hers. "Take care, baby girl."

"I will," she said and leaned into him. She didn't want to tell him about the baby when he was pissed off. She needed to calm him down. God, he would be an absolute pain in the ass when he found out she was pregnant.

"You're not allowed to walk any dog heavier than ten pounds," Gavin snapped.

Lyla sighed. "I'm telling you, this pit bull was adorable. When I passed out, he stayed right by my side."

Gavin ran a hand down his face.

"What, Gavin?"

"He could have killed you!"

"Don't be dramatic," she chided as she sat on his lap, one arm draped over his neck. "I know how to deal with beasts." She wagged her eyebrows at him, but he wasn't amused.

His hand squeezed her hip. "Lyla, I don't know how to tell you this."

"What?"

He wrapped an arm around her waist and squeezed. "Nothing can happen to you."

She softened. "Nothing will."

His hand went to her chest and unerringly found the stab wound inches from her heart. "I've had too many close calls. I want to chain you to the bed with a twenty-four-hour guard, but you won't let me, and you need to live your life. I get that, and I'm trying and..." He turned her, so she straddled his lap and laid his head on her chest. "You're making this damn hard."

Lyla ran her hands through his hair. "I'm fine."

"You have to be."

"We're gonna make it."

He tipped his head back. When Lyla brushed kisses over his face, he closed his eyes, clearly reveling in her love. She wondered if this was how Manny had been with his wife. They stayed like that for long minutes, just holding one another. Slowly, his tension eased. Their meal was forgotten as they took comfort in one another. Lyla stared into his relaxed face and knew it was time.

"I have something for you," she said.

"What?" he asked without opening his eyes.

"Keep your eyes closed. Let me get it."

Gavin's arms loosened, and she scooted off his lap. Her heartbeat began to speed up as she stared at Gavin in candlelight. He was devilishly handsome. He hadn't lost an ounce of the muscle he gained in jail. She loved him—always had and always would. He owned her, heart and soul. It went both ways. His need and vulnerability where she was concerned were obvious not only to her, but everyone else.

Carmen wanted her to announce her pregnancy with rose petals, balloons, or a new lingerie set. That wasn't them. The big society wedding never happened, and that was fine with her. So much of Gavin's life was in the spotlight. These moments were special and poignant. In her eyes, the simpler the better, and Carmen had conceded reluctantly. She took a deep breath and placed the gift bag on his lap. He opened his eyes and looked at the bag and then her.

"What's this?"

She could feel the tears crawling up her throat. She waved a hand. "Just look inside."

Gavin sat up, peered into the bag, and pulled out the small outfit. He frowned, and when he held it up with both hands, the onesie unfolded, showing the message on the front. Gavin didn't react for a moment, and then he erupted from his seat. Any semblance of relaxation vanished. The air crackled around him with manic energy.

"Are you pregnant?"

Lyla nodded and pulled the positive pregnancy test from her pocket and held it out to him. "I took two. They're both positive."

Gavin took the pregnancy test and looked from the white stick to the onesie and back again. The ecstatic look on his face was too much for her. Tears trickled down her cheeks. He tossed everything on the table and hauled her into his arms.

"Thank God. Thank you, thank you," he said into her hair.

"You're happy?" she mumbled into his chest.

"This is the best day of my life." Gavin tilted her chin up and raked her face with assessing eyes. "Are you happy?"

"I'm scared," she whispered.

"And happy?"

"Yes."

He closed his eyes but not before she saw a glimmer of wet. He kissed her, his tongue caressing and claiming before he released her. Lyla stared as he backed up and punched his fist in the air.

"I'm going to be a dad!"

He rushed toward the front door and opened it. She caught a glimpse of Blade's alarmed expression before Gavin shouted the news for his whole security team to hear. Blade smiled and clapped him on the back. After a round of congratulations, Gavin came back inside and rushed toward her. He unbuttoned her shirt and splayed his hands over her slightly rounded stomach.

"Okay, tell me everything," Gavin ordered.

She told him about her sensitive stomach and how Carmen tricked her into taking the pregnancy test. Gavin laughed uproariously.

"Thank God for Carmen," he said. "So you don't know how far along, nothing?"

"No, I have an appointment tomorrow with an obstetrician.

"I'm coming."

"Yes, I want you there." She was terrified. How did single mothers do this? She would demand that Gavin be there every step of the way.

"Nora's coming," Gavin said, running his hands over her scarred abdomen.

"We don't know if it's a girl."

"Then we keep trying until I get my little girl." Gavin caught her in his arms. "Holy shit, I'm happy."

He carried her to the couch and set her on the cushions before he dragged off her shorts and underwear and then his own pants. His cock lay flat against his belly, he was so turned on. He crouched over her, rubbing his dick against her entrance as he kissed her breathless. His hands moved over her, rough and possessive.

"I can't wait," he muttered as he slid inside her. He shuddered and looked down at her like the warrior he was. "You belong to me, Lyla Pyre."

"Every inch," she reassured him.

"Every breath." He brushed his thumb over her bottom lip. "Every moan." He slid out so only the tip of him was inside her and then thrust back in, slow and easy. She caught her breath, and he grinned. "Every smile. Mine."

"And I own you," Lyla declared, wrapping her legs around his waist and forcing him deeper. "You're going to be with me every step of the way. I'm not doing this alone."

"I'm going to be there for everything." He ran his hands down her sides. "You're going to be beautiful pregnant. I know it."

Lyla grimaced. "From what I read today, it's not going to be pretty."

"I'm game, baby."

"I want a dog," she blurted.

He paused. "What?"

"If we have kids, I want a dog. I've always wanted one, but my dad wouldn't let me."

"Then get one," Gavin said carelessly and leaned down to taste her neck. "God, you smell good."

Lyla felt a frisson of excitement and arched her back.

"You're asking for it," he growled.

"Yes, I am," she said in a deliberately breathy voice as she trailed her hand between them and cupped his balls. "Are you going to give it to me?"

Gavin's eyes went blind with animal lust. He sat up and forced her legs to unwind from around him. He draped her legs over his shoulders and fucked her hard. She dug her nails into the cushion beneath her as pleasure ripped through her. He powered into her with short, hard thrusts that shoved her toward climax.

"Come on, baby girl, I want to feel you come."

A wicked finger applied pressure to her clit, and she came with a scream.

"I want my men to hear you," Gavin said as he kept up his rhythm. "Who owns you, Lyla?"

"You do," she panted.

"Yes." Gavin pulled out and wrapped a fist around his cock as he came on her belly. "You're mine."

"I know."

"And this baby binds you to me," he said, massaging his semen into her skin. "You'll never be able to escape me now."

"You have to be the most primitive man on the planet."

"Most men are like me, but they suffocate their beast beneath a layer of politeness and civility. I don't bother."

11

GAVIN

LYLA WAS TRYING to kill him. Gavin paced his office and resisted the urge to go home and spank his wife's rebellious ass. She adopted that fucking pit bull! She had no fear or sense of self-preservation. Blade reassured him that the pit bull acted like a cocker spaniel around his wife, following her everywhere and not showing any signs of aggression, but *hell*! For the past month, she had visited the dog shelter three times a week. She never mentioned the pit bull, so he assumed she listened to him and walked Chihuahuas or some other yappy dog she could easily control. Instead, his wife befriended the most aggressive breed in the shelter. That shouldn't surprise him. Against all the odds, she was with him, a fucking murderer, and he worshipped the ground she walked on. If she decided to shine her light on anything, it would blossom as he had. She had been drawn to this dog from the start, so he wouldn't be able to banish it without his wife raising hell. Fuck! Didn't she understand how much she meant to him?

He slammed his fist against the glass wall of his office and glared out at the red mountains surrounding Las Vegas.

Since Lyla announced her pregnancy, he'd become a fucking savage. He was overprotective, oversexed, and overbearing. Carmen informed him that he was acting like a psycho. The beast he usually kept chained in the deep recesses of his mind prowled on the surface, waiting for something to happen. He was ecstatic about Lyla and the baby. He'd never been so fucking happy in his life, but he was so vulnerable. Everyone knew how he felt about his wife. He couldn't hide it and didn't want to. He was waiting for another attack and couldn't stand the suspense. He'd done too much shit in the underworld for those fuckers to allow him to live a happy, ordinary life. The men who lived in the underworld lived shit lives where paranoia and a lack of empathy kept them alive. They wouldn't let him get away scot-free.

Lyla was four months pregnant, and he could barely contain himself. This weekend was the gender reveal party. He was ninety-nine percent certain the baby was a girl. He prayed every night that Nora would be here soon. Having a girl would be confirmation from God that he was forgiven for his sins. Nora would be his absolution, his redemption. Until then, he was a condemned man.

In jail, he'd contemplated suicide. Pyre Casinos would've continued without him, and Lyla would move on. Everyone connected to him was in danger, and he deserved to die for the shit he'd allowed to happen to those under his protection. A wave of exhaustion had forced him into an uneasy sleep, and that night, he'd dreamed of Nora. Since then, he focused on getting Lyla back and trying to repair what was left of their souls. The feel of Nora's little arms going around him was something he had to experience in this lifetime.

He boxed in the ring every day and ate as much as an athlete training for the Olympics. He made sure Lyla went to the gun range and that he practiced as well. He trained for an attack that he was sure would come. And when it came, he would hit back so hard, no one would dare touch what was his. Those bastards weren't allowed to touch something so pure and beautiful. Lyla and the baby were his to protect, and he would do so with his dying breath. Whatever it cost to keep Lyla and the baby, he would pay.

A cursory knock sounded on his door before Marcus entered. He had a stack of papers in his hand, and he was on the phone. Gavin turned to glare at him as Marcus finished the call.

"Something wrong?" Marcus asked.

"My wife adopted a pit bull," he growled.

Marcus grinned. "From the shelter?"

Know-it-all bastard. "Yes."

Marcus shrugged. "Your wife isn't stupid. She knows what she's doing."

"I know that," Gavin spat. "What do you want?"

"Are you inviting me to the baby gender reveal party?"

"How the fuck do you know all this shit?"

"I have my sources," Marcus said. "So am I invited?"

"You want to go to a baby gender reveal party?"

"It's *your* baby gender reveal party, not some stranger's. Plus, I love your wife—"

"No."

Marcus never failed to push his buttons. Gavin didn't care that there was no sexual attraction between Lyla and Marcus. He didn't like the way Marcus made her laugh or that she allowed him to put a brotherly arm around her. Marcus honestly enjoyed Lyla, but Gavin couldn't stand it, not when he was so on edge. Hearing Marcus say he loved his wife, even jokingly, made his blood pressure rise.

"Fine. I think she's a goddess," Marcus amended.

Gavin crossed his arms. "Not even that."

"God, you're a possessive son of a bitch."

"Yes, I am." He wouldn't apologize for it. Lyla was his.

"Whatever, man. What do you bring to a baby gender reveal party?"

"How the hell do I know?"

"Do you want a boy or girl?"

"Girl."

Marcus blinked. "Why? So you can beat the crap out of any man who tries to date her?"

His stomach clenched. He had been so focused on the image of a little girl that he never considered what would happen when she grew up. Dating? Fuck no.

"Since you want a girl, I'm going Team Boy." Marcus waved the papers. "I need your signature, big guy."

Gavin forced himself to sit when he wanted to pummel someone. "What is it?"

"Contract renewals and my research on building another tower." Marcus set the stack down with a flourish.

Marcus wanted to build another tower that would cater to homeowners. Gavin didn't want to cater to anyone, but Marcus was convinced it would be a great investment for high rollers.

"I'll read your report, but I'm not making any promises," he said as he signed the contracts after a cursory glance.

Vinny had been more laid-back. Marcus wasn't born into the role and was hungry to keep Pyre Casinos at the forefront. He collected business contacts as if they were going out of style and wanted to be involved in everything from housekeeping standards to the safety of the pole dancers in the clubs. Gavin didn't mind since he had no interest in the small details. Marcus excelled at everything he touched and was on top of everything, including his boss.

Gavin had no idea how Marcus had time to monitor his activities when his schedule was jam-packed. Nosy young bastard. On the other hand, Gavin admired Marcus for his fearlessness in business. Marcus had done more to advance Pyre Casinos than Gavin had in the past five years. After he took over the position of crime lord, it became Vinny's job to run Pyre Casinos smoothly.

"When are you going to the boxing ring on Monday?" Marcus asked.

He shouldn't be surprised Marcus knew he boxed every day. His secretary kept a two-hour window open every day, so he could train. If no one was available to train in the ring, he went to the gym.

"I have a lot of meetings in the afternoon, so I'll work out at ten. Why?"

"I think I'll join you."

Gavin hid a wolfish grin. Getting Marcus in the ring might be fun. "I'm looking forward to it. Now, get out of my office."

"See you at the party tomorrow. What time does it start?"

"Noon. Do you know where I live?"

"Of course."

Gavin glared as Marcus snatched the signed papers and exited with a spring in his step. Promoting Marcus was one of the best decisions he ever made, but the damn kid was getting on his nerves. Gavin paced as he read Marcus's proposal and snorted in disgust before he tossed it on his desk. He logged onto his computer and ignored Marcus's email asking if he'd read the proposal yet. He would let him sweat. The proposal was reasonable, ambitious, and brilliant, but he wouldn't tell Marcus that. No, he would let the young bastard quake in his shoes and make him think it was a no go. There were investors waiting for his go-ahead, but he would make them wait.

Gavin made some phone calls and walked through the casino with his head of security. He greeted a high roller who'd occupied the presidential suite for a month and dropped a cool half million daily. Then he went to the bar to have drinks with an old business acquaintance named Harmon who straddled the line between legal and illegal.

"Still no word on the identity of the new crime lord," Harmon said as he sipped Scotch.

"How can that be?" Gavin resisted the urge to smash the delicate crystal glass. "Since when are there such loyal fucks in the underworld?"

"You know there's only one thing that keeps people quiet."

Fear.

"Whoever he is, he's hidden behind many people and names."

"I want to know who he is. I don't care what it costs," Gavin said.

He wouldn't rest until the man who murdered his father and Vinny was dead. The specter that haunted his every waking moment would die. He couldn't live in the same world with that monster lurking in the shadows. He wouldn't give up until the specter's blood coated his hands.

Gavin went back to his office, dissatisfaction eating at his gut. Whoever this guy was, he had everyone by the balls. Why? Was he a dirty cop, politician, or richer than him? Unease made him short-tempered and clipped during the rest of his meetings. When he couldn't take the confines of his office a second longer, he left the casino. On impulse, he requested the escort of a branch of his security that used to deal with the underworld. When he drove out of the casino, he looked in his rearview mirror and saw five SUVs filled with his most lethal men. He couldn't twiddle his thumbs any longer. There was one man who had always been hungry for power, and Gavin knew where he worked.

Gavin parked in front of Vega & Sons, the most successful attorney's office in Las Vegas. He armed himself and walked into the building with five men flanking him while the others waited outside. Gavin walked through the office, which quieted immediately when the workers caught sight of him. Every local knew his face since he had been on the news for suspected criminal activity and murder. Gavin didn't give a fuck. He walked into the executive offices and bypassed the stammering secretary as he entered Paul Vega's office. The old man was on the phone, but he hastily put it down when Gavin entered.

"Gavin," Paul said, running a hand over what little hair he had left. "To what do I owe this honor?"

"Don't fuck with me," Gavin said and didn't stop until he stood beside Paul. He didn't trust the fucker behind his desk. Paul had a gun in his desk just as he did. "I want Rafael."

Paul's expression didn't change. "What?"

His temper snapped. He grabbed fistfuls of Paul's shirt and hauled him out of the chair. He put his face in Paul's and hissed, "You know why."

"Gavin, I don't—"

Gavin withdrew his gun and shoved it under Paul's chin. "Rafael's always wanted the title. He always pushed the limits by coming to my clubs and trying to bribe my men. How many times has he toed the line? How many times did you step in to cover his ass?"

"You think he killed Manny?"

Gavin's finger tightened on the trigger. "Does he have an alibi?"

"Yes."

"What is it?" Gavin hissed.

"He's dead."

Gavin didn't move. "He's what?"

"Rafael was murdered a couple of days before Manny," Paul said, sounding weary instead of frightened.

Gavin released him and watched Paul sink into his chair, looking very much like an old man rather than his father's rival. "Where was he murdered?"

"At his home."

"You know who it was?"

Paul rubbed a shaking hand over his face. "No." The hand lowered, and the eyes that looked up at Gavin were filled with fire. "I was planning a hit on you when I heard Manny and your girl were attacked."

"Who's the new crime lord?"

"Fuck if I know. No one's saying shit."

"You think it's the same killer?"

Paul glared at him. "Rafael was so disfigured I had to identify him from his tattoos. I heard Manny got the same treatment, and your girl got gutted."

"Fucker likes knives," Gavin said in an even tone, but the need to retaliate burned a hole in his chest. "I talked to Harmon today. I've put out a fuck load of money, but no one's talking."

"They will eventually," Paul said and lit a cigarette. "I heard you're married."

Gavin tensed. Even though he and Paul had a common enemy, he still didn't trust him. Bad blood flowed between their families. Despite the Vega's money, connections to the police, and under the table deals with criminals, they hadn't been able to dethrone the Pyres. Paul and his son Rafael took it personally. They had clashed and spilled blood more than once.

Paul blew out smoke. "Heard the gal's a looker. Rafael had a lot to say about her."

The memory of Rafael and Lyla talking in that restaurant still had the power to raise his blood pressure. "If Rafael wasn't already dead, I'd shoot him."

Paul shook his head. "You Pyres are something else. You get so fired up about your women."

It wasn't a secret that Paul Vega had no respect for females. The word was he treated his prostitutes like cattle. According to his father, Paul impregnated countless prostitutes until he got the sons he wanted.

"Stay away from my family," Gavin said.

Paul blew smoke out of his nostrils. "You have nothing I want, Pyre. Not anymore. Now, get out of my office."

Gavin flicked the cigarette from Paul's lips and grabbed him by the throat. Paul's eyes bulged as Gavin applied pressure. He enjoyed the feel of Paul's vocal cords squishing beneath his fingers. It had been too long since he dealt out a punishment. He leaned in close and stared into Paul's panicked eyes.

"I may not be the crime lord anymore, Vega, but you know what I'm capable of, don't you?" Even though Paul nodded vigorously, Gavin didn't release him. "I could break your neck so easily. Don't test me."

When the old man was purple, Gavin let him go. Paul fell to his hands and knees, retching and gasping for air. Gavin stood over him and debated whether to shoot Paul for the hell of it when the door opened behind him. He turned as a skeletal man rushed in. Since his men wouldn't let just anyone into the office, Gavin examined the newcomer and realized it was Paul's younger son.

Gavin gestured to Paul who was gasping like a fish out of water on the floor. "I was just getting reacquainted with your father."

The son said nothing, but his eyes flicked from Paul to Gavin and back again. He didn't say a word, which was wise since one punch would crumple this guy. He was reed thin and had a dainty air about him that neither his father nor brother possessed. It wasn't surprising that this brother held no resemblance to Rafael since they probably had different mothers. To Gavin's knowledge, this nerdy brother wasn't involved in the criminal underworld but was a damn good lawyer.

"What's your name?" Gavin asked into the loaded silence.

The son swallowed hard. "Steven."

"Your father tells me your brother was murdered," Gavin said.

Steven gave him a jerky nod but said nothing. He clasped his hands in front of him. Gavin noted that he was trembling. He hoped Steven had enough dignity not to wet himself.

"You have any leads?"

Steven opened and closed his mouth without uttering a word.

"Spit it out," Gavin said impatiently.

"E-eli Stark."

Everything in him froze. "Eli?"

Steven's eyes fixed on something behind him. It was all the warning he needed. Gavin dodged to the side just as Paul fired his gun. Steven let out a high-pitched scream as the bullet meant for Gavin nicked his arm. Gavin whirled around and shot Paul in the wrist. Paul shouted blasphemies as he dropped his gun and clutched his injured arm. Gavin stalked forward and shot his father's nemesis in the shoulder at point blank range. Paul fell out of his chair and twitched on the ground. Gavin shot him in the thigh for good measure and didn't bother to shut him up since the office was soundproof.

The hair on the nape of his neck rose in warning. Gavin turned and was mildly surprised to see Steven fumbling with a gun. It took him only a split second to aim. One bullet shattered Steven's kneecap. He squealed like a pig and crumpled to the ground, hands hovering over his useless leg. Gavin reloaded his gun and debated whether Steven needed more punishment and if he should let Paul bleed out.

Gavin crouched beside Paul. He welcomed Paul's loathing, and the flicker of fear in Paul's otherwise soulless eyes satisfied him.

"You don't want me to visit you again, do you, Paul?"

Paul bared his teeth. "No."

"Then you'll let me know what you find out about this crime lord, won't you?"

"He killed Rafael!"

"And I'll make sure he dies nice and slow, you got me?"

Even though he was in acute agony, Paul nodded, giving Gavin the right to avenge their loved ones. Gavin rose and strolled over to Steven who wasn't taking the pain well. Tears streamed down his face, and he was pleading for Gavin to call 911. Gavin placed his foot on Steven's shattered knee, and he shut up immediately.

"You got off easy today." He exerted enough pressure to make Steven's eyes roll in their sockets. "You ever pull a gun on me again, it'll be the last thing you ever do. You understand me?"

Steven nodded fervently. Gavin lifted his foot and

allowed Steven to believe that was the end of his punishment for thirty seconds before he belted the lawyer across the face. A sharp crack filled the office as he dislocated Steven's jaw. Steven collapsed against the wall and then slid to the floor.

"Stick to what you know," Gavin advised. "I might call you if I need a good lawyer. Be a good boy, now."

He rose and opened the door to find his men talking loudly, drowning out the sound of the Vega's moans. He closed the door and walked out of the building, discontentment eating at his gut. His men dispersed once they were in the parking lot.

Gavin drove home, his temper nowhere near assuaged by the encounter with the Vega's. Lyla saw Eli Stark at Incognito. The new crime lord couldn't be Eli Stark, could it? Eli had his own code that didn't fit with the savage beating of Raphael and his father. Unless he'd changed since his mother was attacked...

He made it home in record time and wasn't pleased when he heard a deep bark when he walked through the front door. Lyla ran toward him, her delighted face doing crazy things to his insides. She hurled herself at him. She had to stop doing that at some point, but he fucking loved it. He wrapped his arms around her and drank from her mouth. He needed her more than he needed food or water. She was everything to him. Her silver blue eyes were alight with happiness, and his worries fell away as he lost himself in her.

Pregnancy suited her. She had bouts of nausea but vomited only once. Much to his delight, her pregnancy was now obvious. Her slim build made her stomach painfully obvious, and her breasts were swelling and extremely sensitive. Lyla seemed to be shining from the inside out. It made his heart ache.

"How was your day?" she asked, linking her hands behind his neck.

"Fine," he said and looked down at a gray muscled beast.

Dark assessing eyes met his. The dog sniffed his bloody shoes. He tightened his hold on his wife, keeping her airborne and away from the predator watching him so closely. Everything in him wanted to back away, lock Lyla in a room, and get the damn thing out of his house. Why the fuck did he assume she would pick a poodle or something? Fuck. Lyla never did what he expected.

"You see Beau?" Lyla asked and fought to get out of his arms.

He didn't release her. "Can't miss him."

She caught his tone and gave him an exasperated look. "Gavin, I've known Beau for a month. I see him three times a week. He's really great. I couldn't leave him there. He *cries* when I leave. It broke my heart."

Gavin grit his teeth. Another male who had a piece of her heart. He reluctantly released her but kept his hand fisted in the back of her shirt as she leaned down and scratched the beast under the chin. The dog closed his eyes in ecstasy, and Lyla chuckled.

"You're such a sweet boy, aren't you? You're happy here, huh?" Lyla cooed before she turned to him. "Come on, dinner's ready."

He slipped off his shoes but kept his hand on his gun. Lyla walked into the kitchen with the dog happily trotting after her.

"Enjoy the peace and quiet," Lyla advised as she dug into her chicken. "Tomorrow is going to be madness. Carmen says she'll be here with the party planner at seven."

"I'll be in my office."

He had no interest in the decorations and games and shit. He just wanted to know the sex of the baby. It was Carmen's idea to do the baby gender reveal party, and when Lyla agreed, he decided to indulge her. The doctor informed the baker making the cake what the sex of the baby was. If Gavin knew which bakery was making the cake, he would have called because he couldn't stand the suspense. Tomorrow he would know what he was having—Nora or a boy. He thought of Marcus's comment about Nora dating and scowled.

"What is it?" Lyla asked.

"Fucking Marcus." He loathed the small smile that curved her mouth. If Marcus was stupid enough to show up at the boxing ring, he might show him his lethal right hook.

"What about him?" she asked.

"He invited himself to the baby gender reveal party."

"He wants to come? Oh, my gosh. I didn't think about giving him an invitation. He's a man."

"He's a weird bastard." Gavin eyed the dog that looked blissed to be near Lyla's painted pink toenails. "I don't even know how he knew about it."

"Maybe Alice or Janice told him."

He wasn't sure how he felt about Lyla befriending his staff, but the damage was done. Alice and Janice became Lyla's fans when she forced him to attend the Incognito opening and volunteered at the dog shelter. They were becoming quite chummy with Carmen, as well, which could only be a recipe for disaster, but he knew better than to interfere with Lyla's attempts to socialize. At least she was still in his realm, which meant he possessed a modicum of control.

"They'll be here tomorrow?" Gavin asked.

"Yes. Janice and Carmen have been driving the party planner crazy. Some of the volunteers I met at the dog shelter are coming too."

He didn't care who came as long as Lyla was happy and he found out the sex of the baby. On that thought, he smoothed his hands over the loose button up shirt she wore. "How is she?" He would assume the baby was a girl until it was confirmed otherwise.

"She's active today." Lyla waved her hands. "It feels like a weird flutter in my tummy."

"I can't wait for her to kick," he said and pressed a kiss to her belly. He glanced once more at the dog that was doing a good imitation of a furry rug. The dog was obviously house trained and well associated with Lyla. "Do you know the dog's story? Where he came from? Why he was turned in?"

"His name is Beau," Lyla said primly, which made him want to bite her. "I don't know how he came to be there, but he was at the shelter for about a year. He seems uneasy with males, so only women walk him."

"And out of all the dogs, he's the one you wanted?" Beau looked like a freaking tank. If the dog used his teeth and muscle, he could easily take down a full-grown man. "You say he doesn't like men?"

"He shies away from men. I think some asshole must have done something to him. I hope Beau fought back."

Lyla rubbed her foot over the dog's head. Gavin suppressed a snort when the dog's tail began to wag. While Lyla talked about plans for tomorrow, he ate and let the sound of her voice chase away his frustration and rage. Since finding out about the pregnancy, Lyla had become more like her old self. Pregnancy had the desired effect— Lyla looked toward the future with excitement and no small amount of trepidation. He loved the way she clung to him and demanded things from him. Before, she'd been too wary to ask for anything. Now, she called whenever she wanted to, and it eased something inside him. Lyla was settling into married life. He wanted to believe that things could go on as they were, but the grim reality of the past whispered in his ear whenever he wanted to believe in a happily ever after. He didn't deserve Lyla and the miracle in her womb, but he would keep taking everything she had to give.

When he finished his meal, Lyla continued to talk as they headed upstairs. He was *not* happy when the dog followed. When he entered their bedroom, he saw Lyla point at a huge pillow on the floor on her side of the bed. The dog glanced at him before he obeyed, spinning twice on the bed before he lay down with his head on his paws, not taking his eyes off Lyla. Apparently, she couldn't resist the sad puppy dog look. She went on her knees beside the huge dog, making Gavin want to train his gun on it just in case. She whispered to the dog and kissed him on the head before she went into the bathroom. Lyla stripped, and he admired the view before he followed her into the shower. Having his hands on her made the savage beast in his head retreat.

When they toweled off, he nixed the nightgown in favor of feeling her bare skin against his. They climbed into bed. She baby talked to the dog again, and he realized the dog was here to stay because she was besotted.

"Thank you for letting me have Beau," Lyla said, tossing an arm over his chest and snuggling close.

"If I'd known you were going to bring home a sixty-pound beast, I would have laid down some conditions."

"He's a good dog."

"We'll see."

He suppressed a grin when she nibbled on his neck. He liked her bite.

"I love you," she said.

He would never tire of hearing that. It was a gift from God he could never repay. This woman had been created for him, and he would do everything in his power to ensure she left this world knowing she had been loved.

"I love you too much," he said.

Lyla chuckled, and the sound made him hard.

"You can't love me too much."

"I do," he said, dragging her on top of him. He catalogued every precious inch of her exquisite face. If she had the height, she could have been a supermodel, but she didn't use her looks to get what she wanted. She looked beneath the surface as so few people did. "You don't know what I'd do to keep you safe."

Lyla searched his face, and he held his breath. She, more than anyone else, knew how dark and twisted he was. She'd left him twice because of it, and he wouldn't survive a third time.

"I know what you'd do," she said quietly and brushed his hair back. "I just hope you don't have to do it."

If he had a tail, it would have wagged. He craved her touch. He didn't care where she touched him or why. He just wanted her hands on him all the time. It took effort to focus on her words.

"I might have to," he said.

Spectacular blue eyes narrowed. "Why?"

"Because he's still out there."

"But he's been quiet."

"For how long?"

Lyla gripped his hair. He liked the streak of pain.

"You *don't* go looking for him, you understand me?" she hissed.

He caressed her ass and reached down to position his cock between her legs. Before she could wriggle away, he gripped her ass so he could go deep.

"Gavin, stop trying to distract me," she huffed.

He sank his hand into her damp hair and rocked her on him as he forced her lips to his. She tried to resist, but he wouldn't allow her to pull away.

Lyla sank her nails into his chest. "I won't lose you."

"You won't."

The coward who claimed the title of crime lord went after a man in his seventies, a woman, and Rafael Vega. Rafael was mostly talk and usually high or drunk. His security did the dirty work, unlike Gavin. The crime lord no one was willing to give up would die. There was no doubt in Gavin's mind that he would win. Sheer rage trumped the specter's petty personal agenda.

"You promised not to go back to the underworld," Lyla said.

"I'm not. I'm trying to draw him out of it."

"So you can kill him?"

"Of course," he breathed as he planted himself deep. "He'll come back. If not today, then tomorrow or the next day. I need to know who he is."

"I don't like this."

He hated hearing the worry and fear in her voice. Lyla had survived that fucker, but she still had nightmares, though they had grown less frequent. The specter haunted his every waking thought, but that was his cross to bear, not Lyla's.

"Don't worry about it, baby girl. I got this," he said as he sucked on her pink nipples.

Lyla gasped and arched, causing his cock to jerk. He began to move faster, desperate to feel Lyla convulse around him with her silken limbs holding him hostage. There was no sweeter way to go to sleep than with his wife's vagina milking his dick for every last drop of sperm.

"Gavin."

He could see she wanted to discuss the specter, that she wouldn't let it go. He rolled her beneath him and crouched over her as he fucked her. Lyla's lips parted, and her eyes went blind with need.

"I put this in you," he said, rubbing his hands over her belly. "You both belong to me. Nothing will take me from you."

"But Gavin—"

"No." He kissed her long and slow. He loved her taste, her scent, everything about her. "He needs to die."

If he didn't want to know the sex of his child so badly, he would have run like hell. There was an explosions of pink and blue in his home. Glitter banners hung on the walls, balloons covered his ceiling, and everyone wore a bow or bow tie to show which team they were on.

Lyla wore a bow in her hair and a bright pink shirt, clearly declaring herself Team Girl. He allowed Janice to pin a pink bow to his shirt because he sure as fuck wasn't going to pin it in his hair. There were pink and blue cupcakes, napkins, utensils, straws, the works. The men migrated outside while the women chattered inside and played guessing games.

"Hey, boss. You look at the proposal yet?"

Marcus approached wearing a blue shirt and blue bow tie beneath his chin.

"Is that why you decided to come? To bother me?" Gavin asked.

"I knew you wouldn't give me an answer yesterday. So what'd you think?"

"I think it's going to be a tight fit."

"So you read it?"

"Most of it."

Gavin sipped on his pink drink and nearly spit it out when he realized it was pink lemonade. Shit. He put the glass on a passing waiter's tray and snatched a small plate of finger foods while trying not to grimace. This so wasn't his scene. He would feel like an idiot if he weren't looking forward to cutting the three-tier cake that would reveal the baby's sex.

"You have feedback for me?" Marcus bounced on his toes. "I can take it."

Gavin gave him a cool look. "I'll let you know if I have any questions."

Marcus looked crestfallen. If Gavin had a heart, he would have felt a flicker of remorse. He spotted Lyla's mother and scanned the crowd for her father but didn't see him. His sources told him that Pat Dalton got a job at a gas station. Lyla's parents were barely making ends meet, but that wasn't his problem or hers.

Carmen ran toward them. "Come on, it's time!"

Gavin didn't need to be told twice. He shouldered his way through the crowd. The cake was white and decorated with baby shit like bottles, booties, stuffed animals, and blue and pink dots. Lyla's eyes lit up when she saw him. She handed him the knife.

"It's time," she said.

Gavin felt a buzz of adrenaline as he asked Lyla where he should cut. He was dimly aware of camera flashes, Lyla squeezing his arm, and the sound of his heartbeat. He poised the knife above the smooth frosting, closed his eyes for a bare second and said a silent prayer before he cut. He raised the blade, but he couldn't see a speck of cake on it.

"Cut again!" Carmen screamed impatiently.

Hand shaking, he sank the knife home again and lifted a thin slice of cake. His body went numb.

"It's a girl!"

12

LYLA

LYLA FELT like a blimp as she tried to keep up with Alice's fast, energetic pace. It was a daily struggle not to give in to the urge to wear sweatpants and laze around the house. Finding clothes that fit was a bitch. She had complained to Carmen, who took her on a shopping spree two days ago. Gavin put his foot down about her going to the dog shelter, and she had to admit he was right. She wouldn't be able to handle some of the bigger dogs if they decided to yank her along the path, and she couldn't lean over to pick up poop so... yeah. She had to be content with Beau who she took to the gun range and everywhere else possible. He didn't even need a leash. He never left her side, and when she indulged in an afternoon nap, he climbed into bed with her. Of course, she didn't tell Gavin since he still referred to Beau as "dog."

"You were great with the kids yesterday," Alice said enthusiastically.

"They were adorable, but a handful," Lyla agreed.

Although she enjoyed the trip to the school where the volunteers from Pyre Casinos painted, cleaned, and played with the students, she was exhausted. The number of volunteers had tripled in the past months, and Alice was ecstatic.

"The students need better computers, and did you see those desks? They were ancient. The music room had plastic flutes and a beat-up guitar. I wish..." Alice trailed off.

"What?"

"I just want more for the kids, you know? They're satisfied with what they have, but they deserve better."

"I agree. Why don't you ask Gavin for more money to get the kids what they need?"

They passed a poker table full of smokers and women wearing strong perfume. Lyla coughed and waved her hand in front of her face to dispel the noxious odor. Her super smelling nose seemed to get more sensitive by the month. She didn't feel nauseated, but she still had odd cravings. Last night, Gavin watched her eat a cucumber dipped in chocolate with poorly concealed disgust.

"I can't do that," Alice said, twisting her hands together. "I mean, they just created this position, and Mr. Pyre's already put a considerable amount of money in my budget."

"It doesn't hurt to ask," Lyla said as they walked through the employee hallway. Cocktail waitresses, card dealers, spa attendants, security, and other workers acknowledged them with respectful nods as they went about their business.

"Do you really think we can ask for more money?" Alice asked nervously.

"Of course. It's for a good cause."

"I don't want to bother him."

"Come." She took Alice's hand and led her through the maze of back hallways to Gavin's office. When his secretary saw them coming, she picked up the phone, spoke into it, and leaped to her feet. By the time they reached her, she had the door of his office open.

"He's free," his secretary said quickly.

"Thank you," Lyla said with a smile, which she turned on Gavin as he rose from his desk.

She went to him and wasn't surprised when he drew her against him for a deep kiss. If he hadn't made it obvious he was in love with her pregnant body, she would have fallen into a depressed state weeks ago. As it was, Gavin seemed hornier than ever, and it made her feel desired rather than repulsive. When Gavin pulled away, he noticed Alice for the first time.

"I'm here on business," she said and rounded the desk to take a seat beside Alice who looked uneasy.

"Business? Okay. What is it?" Gavin asked.

"Well, it's the school where we volunteered yesterday," Alice said quickly. "The kids need computers, new instruments, and the air conditioning needs to be fixed."

Gavin wore an unreadable expression. Alice's voice went up an octave as her nerves kicked in. She began to talk faster and babble about the lack of water fountains and how some classrooms needed new cubbies. Lyla crossed her legs, drawing Gavin's attention. She licked her lower lip suggestively. His eyes narrowed and Alice's voice got louder and more urgent.

"Do it," Gavin said abruptly.

"What?" Alice asked.

"Give me a figure and we'll do it. That will make Janice happy, right?"

"Y-yes it will."

Alice leaped to her feet and looked on the verge of throwing her arms around Gavin. He gave her a look that clearly stated this was business, and he didn't want or need a hug.

"You're a great man," Alice said with a huge smile.

"Get out of here," he said. "I need to talk to my wife."

Alice gave him a thumbs-up and danced out of the office. He crooked his finger at Lyla, who tried to look innocent. She rose, stopping an arm's length away. She wasn't surprised when he reached out and brought her close so she stood between his knees.

"Did you just bribe me into giving more money to a school?" he asked.

"Maybe."

His hands slid beneath her dress and cupped her ass. "I think I like it. You make my time at work more interesting. Kiss me."

She gave him a long, deep kiss that had his hands slipping beneath her underwear and his fingers sliding into her core. She moaned into his mouth and bucked against his fingers, which slid deeper.

"I need you," he said as he set her on his desk and freed his cock from his pants. He spit on his fingers and pushed them deep. She opened her thighs wide and lifted her ass to take him deeper.

"Holy fuck," he hissed as he withdrew his fingers and replaced it with his cock. "I can't go slow."

"I don't want you to."

He braced his hands flat on the desk and fucked her hard. She moaned and was once again grateful that his office was soundproof. He slid in to the hilt with each thrust, and she tipped her head back in ecstasy. It didn't take long for him to come. When he was finished, he went down on his knees and finished her with his mouth. Her legs were quaking, and his desk was smeared with stuff by the time they were finished.

"You should bribe me more often," he said lazily as she sprawled on his lap.

"Maybe I will."

"You should take it easy," he said and rubbed her swollen tummy. "You've been on the go for weeks. You need to cool it."

That was why she was here. She and Gavin needed alone time. "I know."

He kissed her belly. "She's going to be beautiful."

"I know."

Nora already had her daddy wrapped around her finger. Gavin had been amazing during her pregnancy. He wanted to be involved in everything, much to Carmen's surprise and grudging approval. The nursery was ready, and Lyla had two more months to go. They had a birthing class in a few weeks, and she volleyed between terror and excitement as Nora's due date approached.

Lyla checked herself in Gavin's private bathroom to make sure she looked presentable. Her cheeks were flushed and lips a little swollen, but she could always blame it on her pregnancy. People wouldn't know the difference. She rested a hand on her belly as Nora did somersaults.

"What is it?" Gavin asked sharply when she grabbed the edge of the sink.

"Nothing. She's just really active."

"You should go home and rest."

"I will," she lied and kissed him before she sailed out of his office, high on her climax.

Blade fell into step beside her. He was just as protective and annoying as Gavin and hovered around her as if she were a walking bomb. She smiled at some of the volunteers she recognized and made her way to Marcus's office. His door was open, unlike Gavin's. She had definitely come to appreciate Marcus. He was the yin to Gavin's yang. She couldn't imagine how they ever got along without him. His keen business sense and time management skills left Gavin more time than he'd ever had.

Marcus looked up when she walked in. A broad smile curved his lips. "You look gorgeous!"

She laughed while Blade made a disgusted sound. She gave Marcus a quick hug before he sat on the edge of his desk, eyes sparkling with mischief.

"What can I do for you?" he asked.

"I want Gavin to have a week off," she said.

Marcus didn't even blink. "Okay."

"It's his birthday on Monday. I thought I could steal him away and bring him back to you next week."

Marcus nodded thoughtfully. "That's fine. He doesn't have anything that can't be rescheduled. I can take some of the meetings that shouldn't be put off. Where are you going?"

"California. I rented a yacht."

He gave her a concerned look. "Have you ever been on a boat?"

"Once. I'll be fine. Maybe after the baby comes, you can go on a long vacation."

"What for?"

"To relax?"

Marcus spread his arms wide. "I've been working my ass off to get where I am today. I'm relaxed when I'm at my desk, making decisions and money."

She shook her head. "You businessmen."

Marcus brushed imaginary dirt off his shoulders. "We live for it."

"I hope someone comes along and forces you to take a break."

"You have someone you want me to try out?" Marcus asked, wagging his brows.

"I only know man eaters," she said, and he laughed.

He led her out of his office with a casual arm tossed over her shoulders. Blade looked disapproving, but he *always* looked that way. Lyla let out a grunt as Nora kicked hard. Marcus's easy smile vanished as she clutched her stomach.

"Are you okay?"

"Yeah, she just—" Lyla winced as she kicked again. "She's trying to break out."

"*What?*"

Marcus looked like he might pass out. She grinned, grabbed his hand, and placed it on her tummy. Marcus tried to pull away until he felt the kick. He froze, and his eyes went comically wide.

"Holy crap."

"I know."

She released him and wasn't surprised when his other hand joined the first. He looked almost giddy as he waited and then received another kick.

"Oh, boy, I hope you drive daddy crazy," Marcus whispered to her belly.

"What the fuck!"

Lyla and Marcus turned to see Gavin bearing down on them. Lyla stepped in front of Marcus and headed toward the big boss who made his employees run for cover.

"Nora's kicking," Lyla said.

"And why's he touching you?" Gavin demanded.

She reached up to clasp his face. "Hey, Hulk, he's just feeling her kick."

"You're mine," he hissed.

She sighed. "I couldn't be more yours if you tried. Now, stop making a scene. I needed to talk to Marcus about something."

"Why are you going to him? I can help you with everything!"

"I want to surprise you."

"You know I hate surprises."

She gave him a wounded look. "Even from me?"

Gavin hesitated and then glared at her. "You're trying to manipulate me."

She beamed. "Is it working?"

Gavin jabbed his finger at Marcus. "I'll see you in the ring tomorrow."

"That's fine," Marcus said easily and then compounded his sins by giving Lyla's belly another pat. "I'll see you later, gorgeous."

Lyla dug her hands into his suit when he tried to go after Marcus. "Gavin, seriously."

"He's begging me to end his life."

"Gavin, pay attention."

Feral amber eyes focused on her, and her smile widened. God, Gavin was a possessive psycho. He was a man on the edge, but he always reined it in around her. She couldn't guarantee Marcus's life, but she figured he could handle himself.

"I love you," Lyla said and felt his tension ease. "You come home to me as soon as you can."

"Why?"

"So you can make me yours again."

———

"What the fuck are you doing in California?" Gavin roared.

Lyla held the phone away from her ear as she said, "I wanted to be near the ocean." Well, *on it* if he wanted to get technical. "The jet is waiting for you."

"What the fuck, Lyla?"

"This is my surprise."

"To give me a heart attack? You're in another state!"

"Well, you'd better hurry," she said and winked at Beau, who gave her a chiding look.

She stood on the deck of the yacht and looked out at the ocean. They needed to get away from Vegas and let the water soothe them just for a little while. She packed everything he needed, and the yacht was set. She was happy to note that neither she nor Beau was seasick. She had to throw a crying fit for Blade to keep his mouth shut. If she hadn't been pregnant, she never would have gotten away with it.

It took less than two hours for Gavin to board the yacht. She waited for him with a glass of champagne and sparkling water for herself. His mouth was pressed into a thin line, and although she couldn't see his eyes, she could feel the heat emanating from him.

"You made it in time to see the sunset," she said and handed him the glass.

"Lyla."

"Did you have a nice flight? Mine was a bit bumpy, but—"

"You *flew*?"

Gavin smashed his champagne glass and grabbed her by the shoulders. He gave her a small shake and leaned in close. "Lyla, you don't take off without telling me."

She refused to let him intimidate her. "We needed time away, and it's your birthday next week."

"And I would have come. Just *tell* me. I went home, and you were *gone*!"

She heard the fear in his voice. "You thought I left you?"

Gavin released her and ran both hands through his hair. "I didn't know what to think."

"Didn't you see my card on the bed?"

"No. I realized the house was empty and called your cell."

"Maybe I should have taped the card to the door or something," she mused.

He tore off his sunglasses. "No, you should tell me with your voice, not a fucking card."

"Gavin." She went to him and wrapped her arms around his waist. He glared down at her, and she felt awful. "I didn't think you'd jump to that conclusion. I mean, why would I leave you?"

He didn't answer.

"I'm *not* going to leave you," she said and tugged off his suit jacket so it dropped to the deck. She unbuttoned his shirt halfway, so he could cool off and register the cool breeze. "We needed time together, so I rented the yacht for a week."

She poured him another glass of champagne and pet Beau to reassure him that neither of them was in danger. Gavin took the glass, which she forced him to drink as she stood beside him, looking out at the horizon as the sun set. It took Gavin a half hour to chill. The night was cool but comfortable enough for them to lounge on the deck and listen to the water slosh against the yacht.

"Are you still mad at me?" she asked.

"You're trying to kill me."

She clucked her tongue in disgust. "We're going to have fun. Marcus is going to take care of the meetings that can't be rescheduled, and if there's an emergency, I have your laptop."

"Marcus?"

"Yes. We were talking about this trip when you went psycho on him yesterday."

"I think I broke his jaw."

She sat up. "You what?"

"We boxed. Maybe I should see if he's all right."

"You're damn right you should! Oh, my God, you're such an ass! He's a great COO. Why would you do that?"

"He likes to push my buttons."

"So you break his jaw?"

"I don't know if I did or not. The ambulance came for him. I didn't have a chance to check on his status since I had to take over his meetings for the day. I got your text, asking me to come home early, and I forgot about him."

"You're ridiculous," she snapped and pulled out her cell and called Janice who knew everything. "How's Marcus?"

"He has a concussion and a bunch of bruises, but he's fine," Janice said crisply.

"We just wanted to make sure he's okay. Thanks." Lyla hung up and glared at Gavin. "You gave him a concussion."

"Maybe I should teach him how to box."

"You have a problem!" She got up and walked into the cabin. "Come on, Beau."

Lyla walked into the master bedroom and ignored the romantic meal set up for them. She took a shower in the luxurious bathroom. When she finished, she found Gavin talking on the phone while he stood in front of a row of windows that looked out at their surroundings. She was slightly mollified when she realized he was talking to Marcus. After feeding Beau and making herself a plate from the decadent spread, she settled on the bed.

Gavin hung up the phone and turned to her. "I offered to go back if he's not feeling well, but he's at the office right now."

"He loves his job."

Gavin grunted. "I'm gonna shower."

Lyla watched *Friends* reruns. The yacht tipped from side to side, lulling her into a doze. She had bursts of energy, which quickly faded. She needed this week away from Vegas as much as Gavin did; he just didn't know it. Volunteering, fluctuating hormones, and preparation for the baby were exhausting. She drifted to sleep before Gavin joined her in the bedroom.

Lyla stared at crashing waves. Sea spray landed on her face in a light mist, which made her feel cool and relaxed. She shifted her feet, which sank into fine, warm sand. Someone stroked her hair. She turned her head and saw Manny sitting beside her on a white sand beach. His shirt was unbuttoned halfway down his chest. The gold chains around his neck and rings on each finger glinted in the sun while his bare toes peeked out from his slacks.

Her heart gave a painful twist. Even as she realized this must be a dream, she reached out to touch his face.

"Manny." Her fingers touched skin marred only with age lines. She grasped his hand and buried her face against his warm palm. "I miss you so much."

"I see Gavin listened to me."

She looked up and took in every detail of his face. His chest was damp from the sea spray and humidity.

"Listened to you about what?" she asked.

"Starting a family."

Lyla looked down at her protruding belly covered by a thin sarong. "We're going to name her Nora."

"I know. I'm honored."

She closed her eyes as pain and loss ripped through her. "I wish you were here."

"I am."

She closed her eyes and soaked in his presence. He seemed so real and solid, but even in sleep, she knew the truth.

"I'm happy that you and Gavin finally got your act together."

She let out a choked laugh. "It's an ongoing battle."

"He needs you, Lyla. Don't give up on him."

"I won't," she vowed.

"That's my girl."

She could smell his musky scent now mixed with sunblock and ocean. She saw his gold cane in the sand and smiled.

"I knew you were with me."

She looked up. "What?"

"I felt you grab my hand before I died."

Her breath seized. She dragged herself across the floor with a knife protruding from her chest to be near him. Images from that day began to intrude on the dream. The sound of the waves began to fade. She clutched him desperately.

"Not yet, not yet," she chanted. "I need more time."

"You're so brave, so strong." Manny's voice was a soothing balm to her soul. "No other woman would be able to handle Gavin and the trials you've been through."

"Please don't go," she whispered.

"I'm always with you."

She shook her head as tears poured down her cheeks. "It's not fair."

He cupped her chin. "I'm good, baby girl."

"I'm not." She grasped handfuls of his shirt. "I think about you every day. I miss you so much."

"You need to stay strong. There are more trials to come."

"What?"

"He's still out there, Lyla. He'll come for you and the baby. He won't stop. Keep Nora safe."

"What are you talking about?"

The warmth of the sun faded, and the sky began to darken. Over Manny's shoulder, she saw movement. A man in a black suit and mask stood at the far end of the beach. Her heart leaped into her throat. She clutched at Manny even as the monster reached into his jacket and pulled out a gun.

"Manny!"

She jolted awake, mouth open on a scream. She clapped a hand over her mouth and lay in bed, shaking. Gavin slept with his back to her. Beau padded out of the darkness and nudged her arm with his nose. She slid out of bed, sagged to her knees, wrapped her arms around Beau, and wept silently. She felt as if she had lost Manny all over again.

When she composed herself, she kissed his muzzle and went to pee. Her reflection showed haunted, bloodshot eyes, a pale complexion, and colorless lips. Lyla grabbed a jacket and pulled it on over her tank top and tights before she left the cabin with Beau. It was still dark out. She settled on a deck chair with Beau between her legs, keeping her feet warm as the cool ocean breeze swirled around her.

That had been some dream. How could her mind create something so realistic? The beginning had been good, but the end was a nightmare. *Keep Nora safe.* Lyla wrapped her arms around her stomach. Manny was right. The sadist who stabbed her never intended for her to live. He would come back to finish the job.

Lyla clung to the good parts of the dream, but the bad refused to be ignored. Grief rose so strong, she could barely contain it. Like Carmen, she had lost someone she loved more than herself. There was no coping mechanism. All she could do was focus on little tasks and keep putting one foot in front of the other. Her heart and mind still couldn't accept that Manny was gone. Nora would grow up without knowing Manny or understanding Gavin's overprotectiveness. Lyla refused to allow Nora to feel a modicum of the terror and horror she endured because of the underworld.

On a sudden surge of anger, she went into the cabin and retrieved her gun from her purse. Gavin was trying to lose himself in her and the baby to calm his inner beast. It must be torture to know that the man who killed his cousin and father was still out there.

"Ma'am?"

Lyla blinked up at a crew member.

"Do you want me to take the dog to shore?"

"Uh, yeah, I'll come too," Lyla said, wiping her face and sticking the gun in her pants.

She climbed into a smaller boat with the crew member and Beau. They walked along the shore as the sun came up. Beau raced along the beach before rounding back to her and then taking off again to do his business. There was no one around. The isolation soothed her. She dug her feet into the cold, wet sand and eyed the yacht that bobbed just outside of a cove. After the dry desert air, the ocean breeze felt like heaven. She knotted the arms of her jacket around her neck as she strolled.

On the trip back to the yacht, Lyla groaned when she

saw Blade and Gavin waiting with their arms crossed. Gavin put his hands on her as soon as he could.

"You're not making this easy on me, are you?" Gavin asked as he hauled her aboard.

"Beau had to do his business."

"You should wake me up."

"I have my gun." She brandished it, which made the crew members scatter.

Blade snatched the gun, but of course, the safety was on.

"You shouldn't be handling this unless it's an emergency, especially in your condition," Blade said.

Lyla ignored him and poured water into Beau's doggy bowl.

"Breakfast is ready," Gavin said and gestured to a table full of food.

Blade made himself a plate and retreated inside after shooting her a nasty look. Apparently, Gavin passed the time waiting for her return by chewing him out. Lyla piled her plate high. Despite her unease, she was starved.

"Your eyes are swollen."

She ignored Gavin's quiet observation.

"Are you okay?"

She nodded and continued stuffing her face, hoping he would take the hint. He snatched a Danish out of her hand.

"Lyla, talk to me."

"I'm fine," she said and reached for another Danish, which he took from her as well. "Damn it, Gavin, I'm fine!"

"You're not fine. Normally, you don't carry your gun. Something spooked you. What?"

Obviously, he wasn't going to let this slide. "I had a nightmare."

He searched her eyes intently. "About Dad?"

"Yeah." The silence stretched, and she blurted, "He

warned me that this guy wouldn't stop until he finished the job."

Gavin tensed. "It was a dream, Lyla."

"But you think that too, right? That's why you want me to go to the gun range and why you train? You think he's going to come back."

"I'm not going to let anything happen to you."

"You said you were trying to draw him out of hiding?"

"No one's willing to give him up."

A chill crept up her spine. "Which means he's powerful."

"I'm going to get him."

"You'd better."

Gavin was taken aback by her tone. Her heart still felt as if it was being torn in two. It had been a blessing and a curse to have the dream about Manny. She missed him so much. Was it her overactive, PTSD subconscious making things up or a spiritual intervention?

Lyla leaned forward, hair whipping around her as she glared at her husband. "That fucker doesn't deserve to live. He's not allowed to. You do one more kill, Gavin. I won't feel safe until he's gone."

He was silent for so long that she wondered if she'd said something wrong. He rose, leaned across the table, and kissed her. Just when she was getting into it, he sat with a grin.

She scowled. "What the fuck? I tell you that fucker needs to die and you smile at me?"

"You're a crime lord's wife, all right."

"Former crime lord," she corrected.

He shrugged. "Once a crime lord, always a crime lord. I'm hardwired to take justice into my own hands. My resources and lack of morals make it easy."

Lyla watched the ripple of muscles beneath his tight

shirt. Gavin was a beast. He'd bulked up to ridiculous proportions, and it looked fucking delicious on him. He looked like a UFC fighter. He was ready for war, she realized. He wasn't taking anything for granted. He would fight dirty to keep her and Nora. Lord have mercy on whoever was dumb enough to mess with him. After her experience with the sadist, she wouldn't hesitate to pull the trigger on another human being. She couldn't stand by and watch someone else be taken from her. No fucking way.

"What's the plan?" Gavin asked.

"Plan?" she echoed, trying to get her mind off violence and blood.

"You said I'm free for a week?"

"Yes." She took a calming breath. "It's your birthday in a couple of days. I don't have any plans. I thought we could catch some sun, swim, eat, and chill."

"Sounds good to me." He glanced at Beau who was getting a suntan. "I can't believe you brought that dog on a yacht."

"He'd freak if I left him home for a week." Lyla pointed along the coast. "We can go up and down the coast, or we can go ashore if we're not into it. We can do whatever. No plans."

"No plans sound good."

Lyla beamed. "Yay. Birthday weekend!"

Lyla slumped on the couch and moaned.

Gavin's birthday weekend had been a success. They lazed in the sun, swam, fucked, slept, and ate to their heart's content. Gavin had only picked up his laptop once, and she felt refreshed and ready to rumble when they returned to

Las Vegas. She accompanied Alice to the school where they volunteered armed with new computers, instruments and much more. Janice was there, as were several reporters. Lyla did an impromptu interview, which Janice reassured her had been perfect.

A week ago, she and Gavin attended a birthing class. It had been illuminating, reassuring, and horrifying. She was nervous as hell for labor, but she told herself—and the instructor reiterated multiple times—that women had been doing it since the beginning of time, and she would survive. Just when she thought she couldn't get any bigger, she did. Now, she literally couldn't touch her toes. Even putting on yoga pants was a struggle. It was the final haul, and she was big, miserable, and horny as fuck. Gavin was delighted.

Even now, only four hours after he left, she needed him. God! Lyla put Beau in the backyard, locked the front door, and was about to go upstairs to relieve herself when she remembered Gavin watching the live feed on his desk. What were the chances he was watching her right now? She couldn't call his office to ask him to come home and fuck her, but if he saw it for himself and wanted to join... that was on him.

Lyla shoved a section of the couch in front of one of the cameras. Horniness gave her extra strength. She felt as if her body was on fire. Thank God the weather was cooling, and they were going into the holidays because she would have been miserable during this part of her pregnancy in the summertime. As it was, she wanted the temperature in the house around sixty and broke into a sweat at night. Gavin grumbled when she shirked his body heat. Between the two of them, they generated enough heat to warm people in Russia.

With effort, she stripped off her clothes and lay naked

on the couch. Gavin wouldn't fail to miss that, would he? The message was clear if he didn't have his ear glued to the phone or was attending a meeting. A part of her wondered if Blade had access to the cameras, but her hormones decided it was worth the risk. Blade knew she didn't have plans today, so he had no reason to tap into the feed. She propped herself on some pillows and started slowly, just rubbing her hand over her tummy. Nora was going to be a bruiser. She had her daddy's right hook and made it known that she wanted *out*.

"Six more weeks, love," she murmured to her stomach.

She felt a spurt of impatience and then fear. The nursery was ready, but she didn't know if she liked the lavender walls. Maybe she should have—. Lyla nearly slapped herself. She was supposed to be tempting Gavin to come home to fuck her, not daydream about paint colors on the couch butt naked. She looked up at the camera before she spread her legs, giving him a bird's-eye view of one of his favorite places before she touched her breast and winced. They were ridiculously large and sensitive. How did other women handle huge boobs on a daily basis? She was fine with her normal B's, thank you very much, but this was a bit much for her. Speaking of which, Carmen had taken out her breast implants, which was a shocker. Carmen's look changed so drastically in the past months that she was almost unrecognizable.

Her cell rang in the kitchen. She was going to ignore it, but it could be Gavin. She scowled when she saw Carmen's name. Speak of the devil... To give Gavin more time to stalk her, Lyla answered the phone and resumed her position on the couch.

"How's it going, hot mama?" Carmen asked.

"I'm a fucking horn dog," she moaned.

A pause and then, "Are you a horny toad or fucking a hot dog?"

Lyla snickered. "I'm a horny toad, and I hate it."

"Why? You have a man to fuck."

"Uh, he works."

"So?"

"*So* he can't stay at home on fucking duty. I don't think Marcus is going to accept that excuse."

"Screw Marcus!"

Effectively distracted by the unexpected outburst, she said, "Carmen?"

"What?"

"Did something happen between you two?"

"Why the fuck would it?"

Excitement filled her. "Carmen Pyre!"

"What?"

"Tell me, you discreet slut."

A pause and then, "Something almost happened, but I stopped him."

"Why?"

"*Why?* Because I'm still in love with my husband!"

Lyla closed her eyes as the sound of Carmen's ragged sobs filled the line. It had been two years since Vinny's murder, but Carmen cried as if her heart were breaking. Divorce or falling in love with someone else was one thing. Those were choices. What happened to Carmen was cruel. She didn't get a second chance. One day, Vinny was here, and the next, he wasn't.

"I'm sorry, baby. Do you want me to come over?" Lyla asked and looked down at her naked self.

"While you're horny? I don't think Mom or I can help you," Carmen said, calming slightly.

"Bitch."

Carmen sighed. "I don't feel like myself."

"What do you mean?"

"I knew who I was with Vinny. Now, I keep changing the way I look, hoping my reflection will match how I feel."

Lyla frowned, disturbed by this conversation. "And how do you feel?"

"Dark."

Hence, the black hair and risqué outfits. "Do you want to talk to somebody?"

"I'm talking to you."

"You know what I mean. Like, a professional?"

"Fuck no."

"Then what do you need?"

Carmen hesitated. "The same thing you do, I think."

"What?"

"I need to get laid. Just... get it over with, you know?"

"If you're not feeling it, don't do it for the hell of it."

"We'll see," Carmen said. "I'll see you tomorrow? Shopping and pampering?"

"Yes."

"Okay, preggo, have an awesome fuck."

Lyla tossed the phone and then glared at the camera. For all she knew, Gavin didn't even watch her anymore. Maybe she was performing for no one. In that case... she squeezed her breast and gasped in shock when yellow liquid spurted over her belly.

"What the fuck?"

She wrung her hands before she realized it was probably colostrum. It was normal to start leaking right before the birth. She went into the kitchen to clean herself. Could this *be* any less romantic? Hell, she still needed to get off. Her vagina had a mind of its own, and it wanted to be filled not with her fingers, but with Gavin. Was this what it felt like for men all the time? The inability to think past getting off? God.

She swiped her clothes and stomped upstairs, unwilling to embarrass herself any longer. What if this was all recorded, and Blade could recall it whenever he wanted? Stupid, stupid. These pregnancy hormones clouded common sense. She went to her bathroom and had her hairbrush in hand when the front door slammed. She was torn between relief and mortification. Was it Gavin or Blade? She heard running footsteps and then her name being shouted. Gavin. She tossed the hairbrush on the counter. Gavin walked in with his tie undone and his shirt unbuttoned. He lost his jacket at some point and was already undoing his belt.

"How much did you see?" Lyla asked as he started toward her.

"I saw you move the couch and was gonna call Blade when you started the show. I watched you on my cell as I drove here."

He pushed her against the counter. He went down on his knees, lifted her leg over his shoulder and lapped at her pussy.

"I don't want you to eat me out," she said testily. "I'm already soaked. I want your cock. Fuck me from behind."

His response was a moan. She dug her hands into his hair and pulled until he looked up at her.

"I need to be fucked hard."

"Your wish is my command."

She allowed him to continue tongue fucking her as he stripped off his clothes. When he rose, she braced her elbows on the counter and stuck out her ass. She glared at his amused, self-satisfied expression.

"I think being pregnant suits you. I like you desperate for me."

"This is the only baby you're getting if the last two months are going to be like this."

She grit her teeth when he got down on his knees and kissed her ass. He massaged the large globes and then lapped before he rose and positioned himself behind her. Their eyes met in the mirror. He slicked the head of his cock with her juice, and when he slid it up and down teasingly, she wanted to kill him. She pushed back, taking his cock hostage, and he chuckled, obviously delighted by her aggression. How did other women handle this? If she could, she would demand he fuck her at least five times a day. Maybe more than that. She couldn't ask her mother if she'd been a horny toad when she was pregnant, and this so *wasn't* the time to be thinking about her mother. She reared back to urge him on.

"Fuck," Gavin growled as he powered into her. "I think we should have five kids."

"Your dick might fall off, and I might need to find another man."

She wasn't prepared for the hard slap on her ass. She jolted and then shrieked when he smacked her again, hard enough to make her skin tingle. She looked in the mirror and saw that he was pissed. Seriously?

"Gavin!"

"Don't talk to me about other men," he growled and rubbed his hand over her swollen belly. "Don't you fucking dare."

"It was a joke," she snarled.

"Two things you should never joke with me about. One, other men. Two, leaving me. Pretty simple, baby."

She moaned and moved back against him. "Okay, I won't. Please, I need this."

"Do you like my cock?" he growled as he placed his hands on her shoulders.

"It's perfect," she said with heartfelt honestly.

"Then take it."

She met his eyes in the mirror before he began to pound into her. She spread her legs as he fucked her just the way she needed. She closed her eyes to absorb the feeling of Gavin claiming her, of the pleasure he evoked. It didn't take long for her to climax. When her eyes shot open, she found Gavin watching her in the mirror. His face contorted as he came. He rested his face on her spine and rubbed his hand over her belly.

"I know this isn't easy for you," he said quietly, "but for what it's worth, I'm enjoying your pregnancy."

She snorted and slid out from under him. She cleaned herself with a washcloth, aware of his heated gaze, and winced when she slid on a loosely fitted dress. Even the sensitive contact against her breasts hurt.

"I'm hungry," she announced and walked out of the bathroom.

Gavin cursed as she headed to the kitchen, half convinced she might die if she didn't get food in her body in the next ten minutes. Beau whined by the sliding door. She let him in, and he immediately bumped his head against her side. She grabbed celery sticks and peanut butter and was in the middle of her second when Gavin appeared in shorts and nothing else.

"You're not going back to work?" she asked with her mouth full.

He regarded her sternly. "Have mercy on me. I'm beat."

She offered her half-eaten celery. He stared at it as if it was a stick of dynamite.

"No, thanks. What do you want for dinner?"

"French fries."

"What else?" he asked as he pulled out a salad and sandwich.

"A chocolate shake."

He paused in the act of forking up leafy greens. "What else?"

She considered and added, "Shrimp tempura."

He shook his head. "I'll tell one of the guys to make a food run."

She was over the celery sticks. She searched the fridge and made herself a glass of chocolate milk while Gavin watched. Satisfied for the moment, Lyla waddled over to a chair and put her hands on her belly.

"I'm a sex and food machine!"

"You're almost done," he said and sat at the table with her. "What are you doing tomorrow?"

"Carmen's going to pamper me."

"Good." He pulled out his phone and typed something.

She regarded him for a minute before she said, "How often do you check the cameras?"

He glanced at her and then continued to type. "Once an hour. I can watch from my phone as well."

"Is it recorded?"

"Don't worry. I'll delete it."

13

LYLA

LYLA WIPED sweat from her brow as she finished dressing and sat on the bed. She looked at Beau.

"Pregnancy isn't for pussies," she said.

Beau cocked his head to the side and then ambled over with his tail wagging. He nudged her tummy with his nose and sat. She leaned forward to scratch him under the chin. He closed his eyes in doggy ecstasy, and she covered his face in kisses. She couldn't imagine life without him. Beau seemed to sense her precarious moods and never budged from her side.

"You're such a good boy. You ready to go?"

Carmen called last night and told her they were going to the spa for pampering. She had a pregnancy massage scheduled and could barely contain herself. The past two months of her pregnancy had been hell. Her back ached, she was sleep deprived, and she didn't know her own body anymore. Last night, she went to the bathroom ten times. She didn't know whether she had to pee, poop, or fart. Unable to sleep, she decided to go for a swim at two in the morning. Gavin dozed on a lounge chair as she floated in the heated pool. When she was tired, they went to bed, and she finally slept.

Lyla stood, hands outstretched for balance. She sucked in a breath at a brief flash of pain. She raised her shirt and watched her stomach shift as Nora moved. God, this kid had energy to spare. She fetched her purse and checked her pistol to make sure the safety was on and that she had an extra clip just in case. Since her dream about Manny, she had been on edge. Gavin beefed up her security, but it didn't make her feel safer. She could hear an invisible clock counting down to a showdown she wasn't privy to. Nora would be here soon. Was that what the sadist was waiting for? Fuck that.

"Come on, Beau."

Lyla held the rail as she walked downstairs. Beau trotted by her side as she opened the front door. Their property was always teeming with guards, and today was no exception. Five SUVs lined the drive.

She looked at Blade. "You don't think this is overkill for a trip to the spa?"

"Gavin doesn't think so," Blade said.

No, her husband wouldn't think having a security detail of twenty guards was overkill. "Let's go."

The guards climbed into the SUVs. Lyla and Beau got into the back seat while Blade drove and his second in command, Jordy, rode shotgun. Jordy had a baby face, which was deceiving since he had to be lethal and capable of carrying out brutal tasks if he was in Gavin's employ.

"Where to, Lyla?" Blade asked.

"We have to pick up Carmen and my aunt, and then we're going to the spa," she said.

Beau rested his face on her thigh and closed his eyes as they left the property. Lyla texted Carmen that they were on their way and stroked Beau's head. It had been nine months since Gavin showed up in Montana and married her. Lyla rubbed a hand over her swollen stomach. Of course, Gavin wasn't satisfied with just marrying her. He had to get her pregnant as fast as possible. What had Gavin said when he brought her back? *I need you with me, Lyla. I'll take whatever you give me.* Gavin had, indeed, taken whatever she offered and given back so much more. The strength of his love humbled her. She wouldn't have been able to handle him in her younger years, but everything felt right now. They had been through enough trials to last them a lifetime, and they were still here. They would make it.

Carmen and Aunt Isabel came out to the SUV when they pulled up. Carmen sat in the last row of seats while Aunt Isabel sat on Beau's other side and stroked his back. Aunt Isabel chattered all the way to the spa about the benefits of the wrap she was going to get. She enjoyed spending time with her aunt and cousin. They enjoyed and supported one another. Her mother wanted in on their girl days, but Lyla refused. There would always be drama with her parents, and they would never stop hounding her for money. With her daughter on the way, Lyla wanted all negativity out of her life and that included her parents. She wanted to keep those who loved and cared for her close. Everyone else could go screw themselves.

Lyla sucked in a breath as she stepped down from the SUV. Carmen rubbed Lyla's stomach as if she was a lucky Buddha.

"How's Nora?" Carmen asked.

"Really active today." Lyla winced and arched her back as a sharp pain passed through her belly.

"What is it?"

"Sore today," Lyla said.

"I can't go into the locker room," Blade said in a low voice. "I'll be in the waiting room. You have your phone?"

Lyla checked her purse, nodded, and then kissed Beau. Blade clipped on his leash and went ahead of them as they walked into the spa. Blade settled by the door closest to the locker room after they checked in.

The smell of eucalyptus immediately raised her spirits. Naked women paraded through the locker room with perfect, Barbie-like bodies. Aunt Isabel, Carmen, and Lyla were the only ones without implants. Lyla slipped into a robe, which gaped at the throat, revealing a hint of her scars. The women stared, horrified by her swollen belly and disfigured chest. Lyla ignored them because she was too sore to care. The unrelenting pressure in her pelvis wasn't going away and seemed to be getting heavier by the hour. Would her last two months of pregnancy be like this? She hoped not.

Her therapist was a groovy hippie around her mother's age who made her feel comfortable and safe. The therapist put her on a table with a cutout for her tummy. Lying on her stomach for the first time in months was heaven. She fell asleep ten minutes into the massage and felt like a million dollars when she waddled into her facial. The esthetician was a Thai woman who spoke little English, which suited Lyla just fine since she didn't feel like talking.

Lyla wasn't allowed in the sauna, steam rooms, or Jacuzzi, so she sat on a heated lounger and dozed. Aunt Isabel and Carmen went from treatment to treatment like giddy schoolgirls. They finished their trip with nails and hair. Lyla got a mani and pedi with pink and white designs and a blow out.

"I'm hungry," she announced.

"For what?" Carmen asked.

"Burger and fries."

Carmen shook her head. "You have the worst munchies I've ever seen."

"Wait until it happens to you!" She caught Carmen's almost imperceptible flinch. She put her arm around her cousin. "It could happen."

Carmen took a deep breath. "You know, Vinny wanted kids and I wanted to wait?"

Lyla sighed. "It wasn't meant to be."

"I know."

They walked out of the locker room. Beau jerked out of Blade's hold and ran to Lyla. When she leaned over, he licked her face. She sputtered and laughed.

"I want a burger and fries," she announced to Blade.

"Third time this week," he said without inflection.

"Don't judge me!"

"I'm not judging, I'm making an observation."

She jabbed her finger at him. "You don't need to tell Gavin."

"He wants to know."

"He doesn't need to know everything that I put in my mouth!"

"I follow my orders."

Lyla rolled her eyes as they piled into the SUV and drove to the nearest burger joint. When they reached Aunt Isabel's house, Lyla stretched out on the couch and fell asleep. Two hours later, she woke to the sound of laughing. There was a heavy weight on her ankles. She didn't have to look to know it was Beau. Her lips quirked as she listened to Aunt Isabel and Carmen singing with the radio. She sat up and winced as her womb clenched. She shouldn't have ordered that second burger...

"What is it?"

Lyla turned her head and saw her shadow, Blade. "Did you take a nap?"

"I don't nap."

"When do you sleep?"

"When you do."

She stared at him. "You don't stalk me on the house cameras, do you?"

Before her mind could go nuts about the shit he must see, he shook his head.

"I used to, but I'm not supposed to access the cameras unless there's an emergency." He jerked his head at a diamond studded watch Gavin gave her a couple of months ago. "That watch has a heart monitor so I know when you're sleeping or distressed. It also has a GPS."

"And neither of you thought to tell me this?"

He shrugged. "It's better than following you around the house or sleeping right outside your bedroom. I get alerts when you're asleep or awake. Gavin deactivates it when he's with you." He gave her a piercing look. "Your nightmares are becoming less frequent."

Finding out he was privy to something so private, she paled. She had known Blade just as long as Gavin. Blade had been Gavin's personal bodyguard before he became hers. She spent more time with Blade at her side than Gavin, but she knew next to nothing about him. The day of Manny's murder, Blade had been shot five times and managed to alert Gavin in time to save her life.

"I never thanked you," she said quietly.

He was silent for a moment and then he said, "I did my job."

"Both of us almost died that day."

"I'm sure it won't be the last time I'll be shot."

"Why do you do it?"

"That's my job."

"But why choose this? Is it the money?"

He didn't respond immediately. The smell of fresh baked oatmeal cookies drifted into the living room, stoking Lyla's appetite, but she resisted.

"I threw my life away before I hit puberty. I was a junkie going nowhere when Manny executed everyone in my gang but decided to give me a chance since I was so young. I watched the Pyres take control of all the local gangs." Blade shook his head. "If you think the Pyres are bad, you should see what the local gang lords did to their members. They infected them with HIV, got them hooked on drugs, or made them commit murders to prove their loyalty. If you tried to leave, they raped or killed your wife, mother, neighbor, anyone you cared for. Life means nothing to them. All they care about is territory, respect, and money. The public is fair game. The Pyres put a stop to that. They make it... civilized, if you will." Blade's eyes gleamed. "Yeah, they kill and torture, but only if you're stupid enough to betray them. They don't cut off limbs, pluck out your eyes, or make you watch as your son is bled out in front of you."

Her skin rippled with goose bumps. Blade showed no emotion as he spoke. She stared into fathomless black eyes and could almost hear the echoes of the horrors he had seen. In the kitchen her aunt and cousin began to sing "Gimme More" by Britney Spears.

"I know what the streets used to be like before the Pyres claimed full control. I've known Gavin for over half my life. I taught him how to shoot and fight. He was conditioned to walk into a daily hell and be able to function under pressure. You don't know what Manny did to him to accomplish that."

Beau ducked his head under her arm and nudged her hand. She took a shaky breath and stroked his head.

"Emotion is a sign of weakness in my world. When you started dating, Gavin didn't change so you weren't seen as a weakness to exploit, just a piece of ass."

Lyla gave him a baleful look.

"When you left, Gavin went completely cold and got heavily involved in the underworld dealings. He wasn't like Manny who ran the show and had people carrying out his orders. Gavin got his hands dirty. He dealt with everything personally. Everyone knew his face. The things he did to bring the criminal underclass to heel are legend. He became the most feared man in the state. The fact he could transition from the merciless crime lord to the polished CEO in the boardroom scared the shit out of everyone. When he brought you back, his image began to crack." Blade shook his head. "The filth in the underworld can smell weakness a mile away. Vinny got gunned down, and then you and Manny were attacked."

"So it's my fault?"

"Your effect on Gavin has caused a ripple effect through the city. The underworld is in chaos, and the man who's taken the throne is a sick fuck who encourages chaos and destruction. They lace candy with drugs and hand them out to kids, they slaughter and steal... The new crime lord is good at keeping his identity a secret. So far, all we've been able to discover is that he has a fondness for leaving mutilated victims in his wake."

"So what's the answer?"

Blade's eyes flicked to her stomach and then her eyes. "Most men who have seen what Gavin has can't live normal lives, but he's managed to do so through you. He made his choice. He won't give you up. The whole city could go up in flames, and he wouldn't go back to the underworld if it meant losing you."

"What do I do?"

Blade didn't answer for a long minute. Their gazes held. She gripped the back of Beau's neck as something built inside her.

"I don't know," Blade said finally. "All we can do is hope we can bribe someone to give up the identify of the new crime lord, kill him and hope whoever's next to take the throne isn't as sick as he is."

Lyla moaned as a cramp dragged at her insides.

"What is it?" Blade asked sharply.

"I'm having these pains," she said, and Blade stiffened.

"Are you sure it's not labor?"

"It's probably that Braxton Hicks thing."

"What?"

"False labor." She let out a long breath as it faded. "Damn. It keeps coming and going."

"Like labor?"

She shot him an irritated glance. "Contractions are supposed to be consistent. This has been happening since yesterday. Sometimes I don't feel anything for three or four hours."

"We'd better head home," Blade said and rose.

"I'll say goodbye to Carmen and Aunt Isabel, and then we can go," she said.

Lyla walked slowly toward the kitchen and tried to ignore the ache in her belly. Carmen and Aunt Isabel were dancing in the kitchen while they prepared a casserole. After her talk with Blade, she was glad to see her family so carefree and happy. She couldn't believe how much Aunt Isabel had come out of her shell since Uncle Louie's passing. The longer Aunt Isabel and Carmen were together, the closer they became. Lyla wished she could have that type of relationship with her mother.

"Stay for dinner," Aunt Isabel said.

"I'm not feeling that great, and Gavin will be home soon." Lyla kissed her aunt on the cheek and waited patiently as she stroked her belly.

"You're going to be such a gorgeous girl," Aunt Isabel cooed. "We can't wait for you, Nora. You're so loved."

Lyla blinked back tears. Yes, her baby was going to be loved. Nora wouldn't have Manny or Uncle Louie. Instead, she had Gavin, Blade, and Marcus. It was an interesting mix, but they would dote on her.

"And I'm going to be the coolest aunt ever," Carmen said to Lyla's belly. "I'm going to teach you all the things your mother doesn't want you to know."

Lyla rolled her eyes and kissed Carmen on the cheek. "Thank you for today. It's just what I needed." She caught her breath caught as another pang came and went.

She made her way to the door where Blade waited. He got into the driver's seat while Jordy opened the back door for her and Beau. Lyla shifted restlessly on the seat and couldn't find a comfortable position. If felt as if Nora was doing jumping jacks on her pelvis.

They drove out of Aunt Isabel's neighborhood and emerged on the older side of town. It was run down and not the safest area, but it wasn't completely overrun by crime yet. Maybe Carmen and Aunt Isabel could move closer to her once the baby was born... She spotted a crew of gangsters standing on the corner, and her stomach dipped. Blade painted the underworld in a way that made it so vivid she could feel it pressing in on her. She knew what Gavin was capable of. She'd witnessed him beat that guard to death with such methodical precision that she knew it wasn't his first time. The underworld needed a crime lord, one with a code who could control the sick perverts and sadists.

Beau focused on her as if he could sense her inner turmoil. She let out a long breath and then gripped the door handle as a cramp gripped her uterus in a visc.

"Shit," she hissed.

"What?" Blade asked sharply.

She writhed on the seat. "C-can you pull over?"

"Why?"

"Pull over!" she shouted and put her hands on her belly, which was hard as a rock. "I need to walk. I think sitting is making the cramps worse."

Blade pulled off the main road and followed a small side street to an empty field. She stepped out of the SUV and began to pace. The sun was beginning to set, and the temperature began to drop. Beau nudged her with his nose.

"You okay?" Blade asked.

The other SUVs parked and the guards got out to see what was going on.

"I'm just gonna walk around a little." Beau whined in the back of his throat and stared up at her. "Go run."

Beau hesitated.

"Go on," she said.

Beau darted across the field, his legs a blur. Lyla rubbed her stomach and took a deep breath. They weren't in the best part of town, but with her security, she wasn't worried.

"You should go to the hospital and call Gavin," Blade said.

"I have eight weeks left until my due date."

"You could always have her early."

"No."

He shook his head. "You don't take your health and safety seriously."

"Why should I when I have you and Gavin?"

Blade glared at her, but she thought she saw a glimmer of amusement in his eyes.

"Do you think one life is worth sacrificing to save thousands?" The question popped out of her mouth before she could hold it back.

"It depends on who cares for the life you're sacrificing."

His words hung in the air between them.

"My family was murdered in front of me when I was eight years old. I haven't felt much since then. I thought Manny was the cruelest man I'd ever met until Gavin took over. Those men... I didn't believe they had feelings until you came around. It's the craziest shit I've ever seen. I thought love was a myth made up by people who couldn't face how fucked up the world really is." Blade cast a wary eye around the field. "You and Gavin have been through major shit and put your issues to the side to become a unit. Never seen anything like it in my life."

"And?" She couldn't decipher the expression on his face. It was dark and intense. She wasn't sure if he was pissed, disgusted, or something else entirely.

"I thought the scariest thing in the world was a man with nothing to lose," Blade said.

"It isn't?"

"No, the scariest thing in the world is a man who has everything to lose." He took a deep breath, his big chest expanding as he glared at her. "Never believed in family, loyalty, or love before I watched you and Gavin. What you two have is worth protecting."

Lyla swallowed hard. She and Blade had never been friends. They had always maintained a professional distance. This was the first time he had opened up to her, and it made her mind reel with the knowledge that people could survive such pain and suffering. Gavin and Blade had both been raised to survive in hell and were capable of such brutality yet treated her with care and respect.

She reached out and placed her hand on his arm. She felt his muscles jump beneath her fingers. He jerked, eyes flaring as he stared at her. She opened her mouth to speak, but a strange popping sound made her turn. Blade threw her to the ground. Lyla landed with a jolt and groaned as another pain clutched her stomach.

Blade pulled out his gun and fired. The sound nearly burst her eardrum. She rolled away and looked across the field and couldn't comprehend what she was seeing. Her guards were firing at... each other? There was a gun battle taking place, and they were using the SUVs and trees for cover.

"What the fuck is going on?" she shouted over the gunfire.

Blade didn't answer. He hauled her up, shoved her behind him, and emptied his gun. Two guards dropped. Blade reloaded as he backed up with her behind him. Lyla clutched fistfuls of his suit, unable to comprehend what was happening. Three guards ran forward, guns raised with Jordy leading the pack, eyes cold and blank. Blade shot twice, wounding two but not killing them. Jordy stopped and took aim. A gray shape launched itself out of the darkness. Beau clamped Jordy's arm in his mouth and shook his head savagely. Jordy screamed, firing his gun wildly.

"Beau!" she screamed.

"Let's go!" Blade shouted.

More of her security ran forward. Lyla panicked. She couldn't tell who was trying to defend or kill her. Blade reloaded as he shielded her with his body and killed two security guards who had been with Gavin for over a decade. Blade slapped the keys in her hand and shoved her.

"Get in the SUV and lock the doors. It's bulletproof."

Lyla ran the last few feet to the SUV and ducked as a bullet hit the car less than a foot away. Blade returned fire. She yanked the driver's door open, scrambled into the seat, and slammed the door. The SUV rocked with the force of the bullets imbedding in its side. She tipped sideways with her hands over her head. The glass didn't shatter. Lyla curled around her daughter, wondering if this was it. Through the terror, anger rose. She had to fight back.

Lyla forced herself to sit up and jumped as two men tried the door. Her guards stared at her as if she were something to be annihilated. They began to shoot at point blank range. Lyla put the keys in the ignition and fired up the SUV. Even as she slammed her foot on the gas pedal, the window was splattered with blood as another guard shot her attackers from the back.

The SUV shot forward. She could still hear the ping of bullets, but she ignored them and focused on getting out of the thick of it. When she was on the outskirts of the field, she made a U turn and braked hard. Her breathing was choppy as she flipped on the headlights and blindly reached in the back seat for her purse. She pulled out her gun and fumbled with the controls to move the seat forward as she examined the field. She located Beau who was wrestling with Jordy on the grass. There was a flash as Jordy fired his gun. Beau's body jerked, and her heart stopped as he flopped on the grass. Jordy got to his feet and raised his gun for a killing shot.

"No!" Lyla slammed her foot on the gas.

The SUV kicked up dirt as it lurched forward. Men dodged out of the way as she barreled across the field toward Jordy who swung his head around. Rage obliterated all other emotion. *No.* This couldn't happen to her again. She wouldn't allow it. Beau lay still and lifeless on the dirt, gray coat gleaming with blood.

Jordy fired. His bullet hit the windshield, splintering the glass in front of her, but it didn't shatter. Lyla leaned to the right and kept her eye on her target as he fired again, inches from the last bullet. Jordy turned and fled, but he couldn't outrun her. When the bumper was inches from him, Jordy dodged, but she anticipated that. Lyla turned sharply and hit him. There was a sickening crunch of bones and a strangled cry as she ran him over.

The SUV skidded as she made a sharp turn and paused to take in the scene. Blade hid behind a tree and was being approached from two sides. Lyla slammed her foot on the pedal and went after one of the traitors. He met the same fate as Jordy. Sweat trickled down her forehead as she turned the SUV around again and rolled the window down to take a shot. A traitor screamed as she got him in the gut. That would be a painful death. She swung her gun around when someone pounded on the passenger door and saw Blade. She unlocked the doors, and he hopped in.

"Roll up your window," Blade snapped.

"Is it over?"

"I don't know. Let's get out of here."

"Jordy shot Beau."

"Lyla, we have to go. I don't know who we can trust—"

"I'm not leaving without him!" Lyla drove toward Beau, who hadn't moved. When she tried to get out of the car, Blade clamped a hand on her arm.

"Keep your ass in here!" Blade ordered and got out.

He went to Beau's body and held up his gun when two guards approached. They tossed their guns, and Blade lowered his. She heard low voices, and then the trunk opened.

"Is he alive?" Lyla shouted. She wanted to see and touch, but she couldn't pry her hands off the steering wheel.

"He's breathing," Blade said and slammed the trunk.

The driver's door opened. Lyla raised her gun, and a guard held his hands up.

"I'm not gonna hurt you, I promise," he said, his suit splattered with blood. "I'm gonna drive him to the vet."

"I can drive," she said, voice shaking.

"You need to call the boss. Are you hurt?"

"I-I..." she stammered, unable to get out a word.

"Come on."

The guard pulled her out and helped her into the back seat. Lyla caught a glimpse of Beau in the trunk, and it knocked her out of her shocked state. She dropped the seat and crawled over to him. Her hands hovered over the bullet wounds. He was breathing too hard and fast. Lyla curled herself around him and willed him to live.

"You can't die," she whispered.

Fear gripped her by the throat. Beau was her companion, her friend. He couldn't die. She wouldn't allow it. Lyla ignored the pain ripping through her stomach and hugged him close.

"You can handle this," she whispered, stroking his head. "You were such a brave boy. Mommy loves you so much. Stay with me, Beau. Just stay with me."

The SUV lurched forward, and she clutched Beau. Blade was shouting from the front seat, but she didn't care. The sound of her cell phone broke through her hysteria. Gavin. She scooted toward the back seat where her purse was. She snatched her cell phone and put it up to her ear as she lay beside Beau again.

"Tell me you're okay."

Gavin's voice was guttural. She opened her mouth to speak, but a sob escaped instead. She buried her face in Beau's wet fur and held him. She wanted him to know she was here.

"Lyla, please."

"Beau's hurt," she managed to get out.

She heard him suck in a deep breath.

"I know. Blade told me. Tell me you're okay."

Lyla shook her head. "I-I'm not okay. Why does this keep happening?" A cramp in her belly made her moan. She panted and tried to ignore what was happening to her body. Everything had to wait until she got to the vet.

"I promise I'll get him, baby."

The SUV braked hard, making her slide a foot. The SUV doors opened and shut. Blade opened the trunk, reached for Beau, and dragged his body into his arms. Beau wasn't moving. The other guard helped her out of the trunk. She sagged to the pavement on her hands and knees and breathed through another gut-clenching cramp.

"We're at the vet," she said through gritted teeth as she forced herself up with the phone in her hand.

"Don't get out of the SUV," Gavin ordered.

"Beau needs me."

She stumbled into the reception area, which was in chaos. The other dogs present were in a frenzy over the smell of blood. Blade was in a shouting match with the receptionist, who was wringing her hands. A door opened and a man in jeans and a shirt appeared. Lyla was about to ask if he was the vet when she felt a gush of warmth. She looked down as water pooled around her and another cramp made her whole body shudder.

"This can't be happening," she panted.

Blade placed Beau on the counter and pointed at the guard who came in behind her. "You stay here and make sure that dog doesn't die. I need to get her to the hospital."

"No, I want to stay—" Lyla babbled and was cut off when Blade scooped her up in his arms and ran back to the SUV.

"What the fuck is going on?" Gavin shouted, jolting her since he was on speakerphone.

"Her water broke. She's in labor," Blade said as he placed her in the passenger seat and belted her in. "Sunset is the closest hospital."

"It's too early," Lyla cried when the contraction ebbed so she could speak. "She's not due for eight weeks."

"I'm twenty minutes away," Gavin said, voice tight.

As Blade put the car in gear, another contraction hit. The contractions were coming closer together and each one was stretching out longer.

"Get Carmen on a three-way call. She needs to be there," Lyla said to Gavin.

Blade drove on the freeway, leaning to the right of the distorted part of the windshield so he could see. Lyla held on for dear life. Beau's life hung in the balance, her baby was eight weeks early, and she'd killed three men today. She ground her teeth together as Blade took an exit. She saw the hospital in the distance. Her bad day was far from over. Giving birth, the event she had been dreading and antici- pating for months, was here.

"Gavin?" Carmen said on speaker phone.

"Lyla's in labor. She's going to be at Sunset Hospital," Gavin said.

"I'm on my way," Carmen said and hung up.

"How you doing, baby?" Gavin asked.

"We're at the stoplight before the hospital," she said harshly as she tried to control the pain.

"Good girl."

"Did you send someone to get Jordy a-and the others? They just turned on us, Gavin. I couldn't tell who was who and—"

"Lyla, not now. We'll deal with it later."

Blade circled the hospital and stopped in front of the emergency room. Another contraction hit and she clutched the door handle and console and tried to practice the breathing technique she'd learned, which fucking did nothing to help her focus. She didn't have her baby bag, which Carmen put oils in to help her through labor.

"Holy fuck. I don't think I can walk. Gavin, this is happening too fast. The contractions are too close. She feels like she's right there—" Lyla screamed as another contraction snuck up on her.

When the fog of pain cleared, she saw three men waiting beside the open door with a wheelchair. Blade set her on the seat and accompanied her as they rushed through the emergency room and across the hospital to another wing. Lyla had two more contractions before they reached the delivery room. A doctor she had never seen stuck his fingers up her vagina.

"You're nine centimeters dilated," the doctor said.

"I-I'm eight weeks early," she said.

"The baby will be here very soon."

People were throwing questions at her, but she couldn't focus on anything. The contractions were so close together that she didn't have time to rest in between. They stripped off her bloody clothes and draped her in a hospital gown. They placed her on a bed and put her feet in stirrups.

"My husband—" Lyla began and then fell back on the bed and grasped handfuls of the sheet.

"Lyla, I'm here."

Gavin ran to her side, and she reached for him. "Thank God. Gavin, she's coming. I need—"

Lyla bore down as the contraction obliterated all thought.

"Don't push!" a nurse barked.

Gavin brushed her hair back from her face and kissed her brow. "Hold on, Lyla. Just breathe."

Fear and panic clawed at her throat. This was what she had been waiting for, but now that the moment was here, she wasn't sure she would survive. There was a confused tangle of voices and people looking under her gown and asking questions. Lyla let Gavin handle it as she focused on her body, which felt as if it was trying to destroy itself.

Lyla trembled like a plucked bow and stared up at Gavin as the contraction ebbed. The lethal predator that lurked just beneath the surface stared at her.

"You could have died today," he whispered.

"I didn't."

"But you almost did."

She clutched a handful of his shirt. "Beau has to live. I won't let him die."

"Blade is talking to the vet."

"I want to know—" she began and clenched her teeth as another contraction hit. How did women endure two days of labor? She wasn't sure she could handle another hour. She endured pain like this only a year ago, when the sadist had attacked her. The fear and horror of what occurred on the field amplified her labor pains to unbearable levels.

"Beau is still alive. He's in surgery," Blade reported.

"I need to know he's okay," she cried.

Two nurses shouted in the hallway, and a second later, Carmen appeared with a Taser. She slammed the door and rushed over.

"I made it! How the hell can you be in labor? You left my house two hours ago. Is that blood in your hair?"

"They fucking turned on me—" Lyla began before another contraction took hold.

The doctor came in and measured her.

"You ready to push?"

She was more than ready. She was covered in sweat and shaking like crazy. Carmen stood one side, Gavin on the other, while Blade guarded the door. Lyla stared at the ceiling and tried to get into the headspace that would allow her to focus beyond the pain. Today had been a shit day full of death, fear, and desperation. Tears leaked out of the corner of her eyes as she squeezed two of her best friend's hands.

"Lyla, when the next contraction comes, you have to push," the doctor said.

She nodded and took deep breaths. Her womb tightened, and she leaned forward and bore down. She stared at the doctor positioned between her legs. She listened to him count and fell back on the raised bed when the contraction passed.

"You're doing great, Lyla," the doctor praised.

"Holy shit," Carmen said and rubbed her arm. "You're almost there."

Gavin's face was closed off. There was a battle taking place in him. She knew all too well what it was. It had been a shit day for him too. Of course, the underworld chose today to rise up and make a mark against them. Nora's birth would forever be tainted by Gavin's old life and nemesis.

"Here we go," the doctor warned.

Lyla felt the contraction coming and met Gavin's eyes. On a day like today, they needed something like this to remind them that life would go on. Pain eclipsed all else.

She bore down and pushed for all she was worth. She felt as if her vagina was ripping in half... and then it was done.

Her ears rang as the doctor placed a small bundle on her chest. The baby began to change color right before her eyes. Nora clawed the empty air and burrowed close for warmth, screaming at the top of her lungs.

The nurses took Nora briefly to clean and weigh her and then placed the baby on Lyla's chest. Despite being eight weeks early, Nora was a healthy six pounds, four ounces. She had a head full of black hair, and when her eyes opened, they all saw the flash of bright blue. Gavin placed his hand on Nora's back. His daughter could fit on his palm. Something elemental moved through her as she registered that she was now a mother.

When the medical personnel cleared out, leaving Blade, Carmen, Lyla and Gavin, there was a strained silence.

"What the fuck happened?" Lyla whispered hoarsely. She felt numb from today's events and couldn't stop shaking.

Blade widened his stance and clasped his hands behind his back. "The men were bribed by the new crime lord. The mission was to kill Lyla. Eight switched sides. We lost two men. All the traitors are dead."

"Identity of the new crime lord?" Gavin asked, his voice as calm as could be, but the air around him sizzled with rage.

Blade shook his head. Carmen opened her mouth and then closed it. Lyla's throat burned with the need to rage. She buried her face against Nora's soft skin and absorbed the feel of her. Nora was so small and defenseless and had been so close to dying today. There was so much hate and evil in the world. She and Gavin were Nora's only defense against the darkness waiting for her.

Tears streamed down her face as she listened to Nora's quick breaths. Tiny hands gripped her hair as Nora nuzzled close. This was her child to protect, and she would do so. Lyla rested Nora on her shoulder and looked at Gavin who was watching her.

Tears trickled down her face, but her voice was steady as she said, "You go back into the underworld, you find him, and you kill that fucker slowly."

CRIME LORD SERIES

Thank you for reading Recaptured by the Crime Lord. Lyla and Gavin's story continues in Once A Crime Lord!

I've written a bonus clip, a glimpse of Lyla and Gavin's first encounter from Gavin's POV. Join the newsletter and have it sent to your inbox!

AUTHOR'S NOTE

Hi All,

I hope you enjoyed Recaptured by the Crime Lord. Please leave a review and recommend the book to a friend, it helps me out a lot!

I really enjoyed writing from Gavin's point of view in this book and hope to do so in the future. Their relationship is raw and full of love and desperation. I hope you've enjoyed the journey as much as I have.

I've written a bonus clip, a glimpse of Lyla and Gavin's first encounter from Gavin's POV. Join the newsletter and have it sent to your inbox!

Don't miss the third installment of Lyla and Gavin's story, Once A Crime Lord!

Mia

BOOKS BY MIA KNIGHT

Crime Lord's Captive

Recaptured by the Crime Lord

Once A Crime Lord

Awakened by Sin

ABOUT THE AUTHOR

Mia lives in her head and is shadowed by her dogs who don't judge when she cries and laughs with imaginary characters. Mia comes from a big, conservative family that doesn't know how to handle her eccentricities, but with encouragement from her fans, has found the courage to put the characters in her head on paper.

Stalk Mia
Website
Email
Mia Knight's Captives (Facebook Group)

facebook.com/miaknightbooks

twitter.com/authormiaknight

goodreads.com/authormiaknight

bookbub.com/profile/mia-knight

Made in the USA
Columbia, SC
18 July 2018